"I Should Be Married And At My Wedding Reception Right This Minute!"

Julie shouted at Flint. "You cannot kiss me. No."

"Darlin', I wasn't the only one doing the kissing."

"Don't call me darlin'. I'm not your darlin'. I'm about to become Mrs. Robert Allen Newly."

"*Newly?* Julie *Newly?*" A snort of laughter exploded from him.

She bopped him on the shoulder with her fist. "Don't you dare laugh. Yes, I'll be Julie Newly, and it's not funny. And if you know what's good for you, Flint Durham, you'll take me back to my wedding ceremony right this minute."

Dear Reader,

The holidays are always a busy time of year, and this year is no exception! Our "banquet table" is chock-full of delectable stories by some of your favorite authors.

November is a time to come home again—and come back to the miniseries you love. Dixie Browning continues her TALL, DARK AND HANDSOME series with *Stryker's Wife*, which is Dixie's 60th book! This MAN OF THE MONTH is a reluctant bachelor you won't be able to resist! Fall in love with a footloose cowboy in *Cowboy Pride,* book five of Anne McAllister's CODE OF THE WEST series. Be enthralled by *Abbie and the Cowboy*—the conclusion to the THREE WEDDINGS AND A GIFT miniseries by Cathie Linz.

And what would the season be without HOLIDAY HONEYMOONS? You won't want to miss the second book in this cross-line continuity series by reader favorites Merline Lovelace and Carole Buck. This month, it's a delightful wedding mix-up with *Wrong Bride, Right Groom* by Merline Lovelace.

And that's not all! *In Roared Flint* is a secret baby tale by RITA Award winner Jan Hudson. And Pamela Ingrahm has created an adorable opposites-attract story in *The Bride Wore Tie-Dye.*

So, grab a book and give *yourself* a treat in the middle of all the holiday rushing. You'll be glad you did.

Happy reading!

Lucia Macro

Senior Editor
and the editors of Silhouette Desire

Please address questions and book requests to:
Silhouette Reader Service
U.S.: 3010 Walden Ave., P.O. Box 1325, Buffalo, NY 14269
Canadian: P.O. Box 609, Fort Erie, Ont. L2A 5X3

JAN HUDSON
IN ROARED FLINT

SILHOUETTE *Desire*®
Published by Silhouette Books
America's Publisher of Contemporary Romance

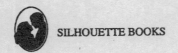 SILHOUETTE BOOKS

ISBN 0-373-76035-3

IN ROARED FLINT

Printed in U.S.A.

JAN HUDSON,

a winner of the Romance Writers of America RITA Award, is a native Texan who lives with her husband in historically rich Nacogdoches, the oldest town in Texas. Formerly a licensed psychologist, she taught college psychology for over a decade before becoming a full-time author. Jan loves to write fast-paced stories laced with humor, fantasy and adventure, using bold characters who reach beyond the mundane and celebrate life.

For Alex Thorleifson.
Thanks for friendship and
for Garner Valley.

One

Flint Durham was back.

A fury of emotions surged through Julie Travis Stevens as she clutched the lace curtains of her upstairs bedroom and watched him rip down Travis Boulevard toward the house.

Dressed in black and astride a Harley, he was roaring in the same way he'd roared out six years before. An unforgettable aura of dark intensity and menacing allure rode with him like a familiar. Unshaven, with a red bandanna on his head and his long black hair streaming behind him, he exuded a wild sensuality that was every mother's nightmare. And every daughter's secret dream.

Squeezing her lids tightly shut, Julie prayed that her eyes had deceived her, that her mind had conjured up an apparition. *Oh, please, God. No. Not Flint. Not now. Not today.* But when she opened her eyes, there he was—unmistakably real.

After six long years, why had he picked *today* of all days to come back?

One thing she knew for sure: Flint Durham was up to no good. A sick, sinking feeling gripped her stomach, and she groaned involuntarily.

"Julie, what's wrong?" her younger sister, Melissa, asked. She gathered her long shirt and crossed the room to peer out the window. "You look like you've seen a— Holy horse patties!" She grabbed Julie's arm in a death grip, and her eyes bugged out like a bullfrog's. "Would you look at that? I can't believe it. It's *him.* It's Flint. Flint Durham. Holy horse patties!"

Julie fought back the panic building inside her as she watched him roll to a stop behind the caterer's truck and set the kickstand. Sure that she teetered on the edge of screaming hysteria, she clung to the shreds of her self-control as he came up the walk, his broad shoulders and long legs moving with the familiar, confident swagger that always had women in six counties swooning over him.

"Julie, he's coming to the door," Melissa said, her voice an octave higher. "What are you going to do?"

"If I had a gun, I'd shoot the bastard!"

The doorbell rang, and the melodious chimes above the double staircase reverberated throughout the big house like a disaster knell.

"Aren't you even going to talk to him?" Melissa asked.

"No way. I'm not letting him ruin two wedding days for me. Hand me my veil before you completely mangle it, and go downstairs and tell Rosie not to let him in."

Melissa sighed. "Why do I have the feeling that getting rid of Flint won't be easy?"

"Tell him that I said, 'Drop dead.' That ought to do the trick. If not, call Uncle Hiram." Uncle Hiram, the eldest of the town founder's four grandsons, was the police chief in Travis Creek, and he ruled the small East Texas town with an iron fist. Uncle Edgar owned the *Travis Creek Times*; her daddy was the president of the bank. And Uncle William ... well, Uncle William drank.

After Melissa hurried out, Julie sat down at her dressing table to finish her hair and makeup. She hummed loudly to drown out the ruckus downstairs. In exactly one hour and forty-eight minutes, she would say "I do" with Dr. Robert Allen Newly in her parents' rose garden. And she was determined that nothing was going to spoil this day. Her pale peach dress was perfect; the weather was perfect; the roses were perfect. Rob was the perfect husband for her. Her parents said so frequently.

The only thing about her wedding that caused her the least bit of trepidation was that her name would be Julie Newly. It sounded like part of a bad jingle.

She would have to sign her letters: Yours truly, Julie Newly.

Shouting from downstairs stabbed at her composure, but she hummed louder.

Yes, Rob was a wonderful man. From a fine family. With a marvelous future as a physician. Perhaps if she'd known him when he was choosing his specialty she might have steered him toward heart surgery or even dermatology, but people needed proctologists, too, she told herself.

And what did a little bald spot matter when he was so good with the children? Perhaps his kisses didn't exactly blister her nail polish, but she'd learned the hard way that other things were more important than wild, mindless passion. Rob was a man of character and substance, steady as a rock. Perfect.

Rob adored her. And best of all, his new practice was in Plano, north of Dallas. She and the children would be out of her parents' house and into one of their own, one too far away for doting grandparents to hover over the kids and continue to spoil them rotten.

Julie heard the front door slam, but the ruckus downstairs continued—the doorbell chimed incessantly amid shouting and banging. She hummed louder and closed one eyelid to put on eyeliner. Her hand shook so badly that the line looked like rick-rack.

"Dammit!" She threw down the pencil and wiped her lid with a tissue.

Melissa ran into the room. "The man is crazy. Wild. I don't know what to do. He says he won't go away until he talks to you."

"Call Uncle Hiram."

"Oh, Julie, are you sure? Can't you at least talk to him? God, he's such a hunk." Melissa sighed and hung on to one of the posts of the cherry four-poster.

A spray of gravel clattered against Julie's window and Flint bellowed her name from down below.

"Mommy, Mommy," Megan said as she ran in the room, grabbed Julie around the legs and plastered her small body against her mother. "There's a man yelling downstairs. And he looks mean. I'm scared."

"I'm not scared," said Jason, Megan's twin brother. He puffed out his thin five-year-old chest as he marched in. "I'll morph into a Power Ranger and kick his lights out."

Julie knelt and gathered the twins to her. She kissed Megan's forehead. "Darlings, there's no reason to be afraid. Aunt Missy is calling the police right now," she said, then looked pointedly at Melissa. "Aren't you?"

"Right this minute. See?" Melissa snatched up the phone and reported the disturbance to Uncle Hiram. "Someone will be right here."

Julie gave each of the children a hug. "Now why don't you run along with Aunt Missy and get your wedding clothes on? The guests will be arriving soon."

Melissa herded the kids out, and just as the door closed, another clatter of gravel hit the window. Flint bellowed her name. Furious, Julie stomped to the window, threw up the sash and poked her head out.

"Dammit, Flint Durham, would you shut up! You're making a spectacle of yourself."

Flint dropped the handful of pebbles he held and looked up. When he spotted Julie, his usual insolent scowl changed immediately into a broad smile with the power of a nuclear reactor.

"Hi, Julie. I'm back."

"Well, isn't that just ducky? Now go away!"

"But, Julie, I have to talk to you."

"I don't want to hear anything you have to say. Go away! Melissa has called the police, and they'll be here any minute."

"Dammit, I'm not leaving until I talk to you!" He grabbed a limb of the oak tree that grew near her window, swung himself up and began climbing.

She shrieked, grabbed a vase of roses and upended flowers and water on him. It had the same effect as pouring gasoline on a fire. He roared, cursed and kept climbing.

She threw everything at him that she could get her hands on, pelting him with a jar of face cream, a candy dish, a pair of bookends. He dodged every missile and kept climbing. She took careful aim at the motorcycle emblazoned across the black T-shirt he wore and hurled a Waterford clock at his chest. It hit dead on target.

A thud, a loud *ooofff,* a curse. He lost his grip and fell, flailing and still cursing, to the grass below.

Momentarily panicked, Julie leaned out the window and looked down to where Flint lay. He didn't move. His eyes were closed. Dear Lord, had she killed him?

One black eye opened. It zeroed in on her. "Now what did you go and do that for? I just wanted to talk to you."

"We have nothing to say, Flint Durham." As she slammed down the window, a siren wailed from the police car racing toward the house. She turned her back and walked away.

Once more she sat down at her dressing table and hummed very loudly.

"Mommy, Mommy!" Megan and Jason came tearing in her room with Melissa chasing after them, trying to tie Megan's sash.

"The policemen are taking the mean man away," Meg said.

"And one of them is riding his *biiig* motorcycle. Wow! Someday I'm gonna have a motorcycle like that," Jason chimed in. *"Buddennn, buddennn."* He made motor sounds and ran around the room holding imaginary handlebars.

"Not in my lifetime," Julie told him. "Now run along and finish getting dressed. Mommy has to put on her wedding gown."

At three o'clock on the last Saturday in April, the guests were assembled on rented chairs in the garden. Since this was Julie's "second" marriage, the ceremony was kept small and intimate with only about fifty people present, mostly relatives along with a few very old friends.

Her favorite Uncle William sat on the second row, slighted potted Julie was sure, looking gloomy. Uncle William was the only one in the family who thought her marriage to Rob was a mistake. Perhaps because Rob was a teetotaler.

Although, by the end of April, the azaleas and the early spring bulbs were long past their season, Patricia Spalding Travis, Julie's mother, in conference with God and three gardeners for the past two months, had seen to it that the garden resembled a fairyland of flowers, and the gazebo fairly dripped greenery and blossoms.

With the elderly Millicent Wall on the harp and her older sister, Eugenia, on the flute, magnificent wedding music rippled and trilled over the shaded grounds. The Methodist minister stood on the top step of the gazebo. Rob and his cousin stood two steps down, waiting.

Julie's palms were decidedly damp. She clutched her bouquet and her father's arm tightly.

George Travis smiled and patted Julie's hand. "Nervous?"

"Extremely."

Her father smiled again. "Rob is a fine man. Your mother and I couldn't have picked a better husband for you or a father for the twins. There's nothing for you to be nervous about."

Julie knew that her father wouldn't be so calm if he'd known about Flint's visit earlier. Thankfully, her parents had been away from the house on last-minute errands. Just hearing Flint's name was enough to dispatch her mother to bed with a migraine and launch her father into a tirade that sent his blood pressure soaring.

She took a deep breath and focused her attention on the ceremony. Her wedding day should be a joyous occasion. She was determined not to let anything taint it.

Megan and Jason led the procession. Jason carried a pillow with gold wedding rings tied securely atop it. An oddly shaped lump protruded from the back pocket of his navy suit, distorting the lines of the tailored jacket. As he had been instructed a score of times, he walked very slowly and carefully, the tip of his tongue at the corner of his mouth as he concentrated on his task. Only once did he swipe his nose with his sleeve.

Megan, wearing ruffled socks and with sash slightly askew, carried a small basket and exuberantly scattered petals from her grandmother's prize Peace roses along the newly laid flagstone path to the gazebo. Distressed that she misjudged and had run out of petals before she reached her destination, she backtracked and grabbed a few handfuls from the pathway to replenish her basket. These she dispensed sparingly until she reached the gazebo.

Watching her children, Julie smiled and her chest swelled with pride and love for the pair. Megan and Jason were the light of her life and worth every ounce of heartache she had endured.

When Melissa reached the gazebo, the music changed subtly. The crowd rose and turned.

"That's our cue, sweetheart." George Travis kissed his daughter's cheek.

Julie took a deep breath, plastered a smile on her shaky lips and they started the walk down the flagstone path. Every muscle in her body seemed to quiver, and once she almost stumbled. Her father patted her hand and held his over it.

Why was she so nervous?

She looked at Rob, who waited for her at the gazebo, an adoring expression on his face, his eyes shining brightly as he watched her approach. He was such a dear, sweet man. How could anybody not love him?

They stopped and the minister began. His words echoed vaguely in the buzzing inside her head.

"Her mother and I do," her father said, then stepped back to take his place on the front row.

The minister began again, and the buzzing in her head grew louder and louder until it was a roar. Was she about to faint?

The roar grew louder. Distracted, the minister stopped and looked up from his prayer book. The guests fidgeted and murmured. Rob glanced over his shoulder and frowned. Julie glanced over her shoulder and almost had a heart attack.

Flint Durham, astride his Harley, vroommed through the side yard, cut a swath across Patricia Spalding Travis's bed of lavender petunias, and was headed down the flagstone path straight for the gazebo.

He screeched to a stop mere inches from the bride and groom, set one black-booted foot on the ground and scowled. "What in the hell do you think you're doing?" he growled at Julie.

The guests gasped.

"Getting married," she enunciated distinctly.

Flint's black eyes swept over Rob, then he sneered. "To *him?* Like hell you are!"

"Flint, would you go away! You're making a spectacle of yourself and ruining my wedding!"

"Damned right. You're coming with me. Get on the bike."

"I will not!"

"Now see here," Rob said, stepping forward.

Flint reached beneath his leather vest, whipped out a gun and shoved it against Rob's nose.

Rob froze.

The guests gasped louder.

A woman shrieked.

A man's voice boomed.

"Mommy! Mommy!"

Panic rose up in Julie's throat. He'd gone mad, absolutely mad. Dangerously mad.

"Get on the bike," Flint said gruffly, ordering Julie with a quick gesture of his head.

"Flint, please, can't we—"

"On the bike." He gestured with his head again. The gun under Rob's nose lifted him until he was tiptoeing in his patent leather shoes and sweating profusely.

"Mommy! Mommy!"

She hesitated only a millisecond. Her babies. She had to protect her babies. She tossed Melissa her bouquet, hitched up the short train of her dress and climbed on behind him.

Flint flashed Rob a wolfish grin. "So long, sucker." He shot the groom with two good squirts from the water pistol he held, then revved up the bike and took off across the marigold bed.

With Julie cursing and beating her fists on his back and pandemonium breaking loose behind them, he threw back his head and laughed.

Two

***

"**D**amn you, Flint Durham!" Julie shrieked, beating against his back with her fist. "Stop and let me off this thing."

"No way," Flint shouted over his shoulder.

"If you don't let me off, I'll jump!"

"You'll break your beautiful neck. Hang on," he said, rounding a corner at a high speed.

She clutched his waist and leaned into the turn, instinctively recalling the technique even though she hadn't been on a motorcycle in more than six years—not since Flint left. His long hair fluttered against her face and she automatically moved closer to him to avoid it, pressing her cheek against his broad back. It

felt excruciatingly, maddeningly familiar. She stiffened.

She would not be drawn into his spell. Not today.
Not ever again.

She began beating his back with her fists once more.
"Stop! Stop! Let me off."

"No!"

Julie couldn't recall feeling so helpless. The feeling
infuriated her. Sooner or later he had to stop—for a
light, a stop sign, or something—and she would jump
off this infernal contraption and call the police. Flint
would never see daylight again. He would rot in jail.

But he didn't stop. He didn't even slow down. Like
one blessed, he hit every light perfectly as they roared
out of town, her wedding dress hitched up to her
thighs and billowing behind her. She frantically tried
to signal other cars, people at a road-side fruit stand;
they all smiled and waved back.

Flint turned off the main highway onto a second-
ary road that cut through the heavily forested area and
headed in the direction of the huge Sam Rayburn
Lake. Oh, dear Lord, nobody knew this backwoods
part of the county as well as Flint did. He'd grown up
on the banks of the lake and explored every pig trail in
the woods. Even if Uncle Hiram came after her with
a posse, they'd never find her if Flint didn't want her
to be found.

They took another fork, then another, in such a
convoluted route that Julie was soon hopelessly lost.

She leaned her forehead against Flint's back and her shoulders sagged. "Please stop. Please, Flint, please."

The Harley slowed, rounded a curve, then drew to a halt in front of a cedar cabin beside the water.

Julie scrambled off the back of the bike and made a dash for the road. His arm hooked her waist and lifted her from her feet. "Not so fast, love. We have to talk."

"Talk? You must be kidding. I don't have a thing to say to you! Put me down right this minute, or I'll scream my head off."

"Scream away, darlin'. There's not a soul within hearing distance." He started toward the door of the weathered cabin.

She tried peeling his arm from her waist. "Please, Flint. You're hurting me."

Looking contrite, he immediately set her down. "Oh, sugar, I'm sorry."

The minute her feet hit the ground, she made a dash for it. Before she'd gone two steps, he caught her wrist. "Hold it. I told you that we have to talk."

He tried pulling her toward him, but Julie set her jaw and dug in her heels—literally—sinking the backs of her peach-colored silk shoes into the spongy ground and giving him a venomous look. He wasn't deterred for more than five seconds. He merely plucked her from her pumps, tossed her over his shoulder and headed up the steps to the porch.

"Dammit, Flint, don't do this!"

He unlocked the front door, kicked it shut behind them, then set her on her feet. When she made a lunge for the door, he grabbed her again. This time he turned the key in the dead bolt and dropped it in his pocket. She struggled against his grip on her, and he let her go.

Glaring at him, she stomped to the front door and rattled the knob. Locked, of course. "Give me the key."

Flint leaned against the mantel of the stone fireplace, folded his arms and slowly shook his head.

"There must be another door to this place."

He gestured to the rear where the kitchen was. "It's locked, too."

Thrusting out her jaw, she declared, "Very well. I'll use a window."

"Be my guest."

Marching to a window, she threw open the sash and met burglar bars. She rattled them. Locked. She whirled and glared at him some more. "Exactly what do you expect to accomplish by keeping me a prisoner here?"

"I expect to talk you. I told you that earlier. I'm determined that we're going to get some things straightened out here, come hell or high water. Just listen to me for a few minutes. It's important for you to understand—"

"I'm not listening to you, Flint Durham," she shouted, covering her ears with her hands and marching around in circles. "I'm not listening to a single syllable that you have to say." Keeping her hands over her ears, she started singing "Dixie" at the top of her lungs as she continued her barefoot stomping.

Flint grabbed her in the middle of a loud "look away" and plunked her into a large leather recliner. "Lord, woman, you don't make this easy. Would you stay put for five minutes. I have something to show you."

"I don't want to see it."

She scrambled up from the deep chair, and he shoved her back down. She popped up; he shoved down.

"Dammit, Julie! Can't you just give me thirty seconds?" He pushed her into the recliner, then quickly lifted one heavy chair leg, crammed the tail of her dress under it and dropped the weight of the chair down on the yards of peach silk.

When she tried to get up, her caught dress held her down. She yanked and yanked, but she was pulling against her own weight, and she couldn't get enough leverage to move and lift the chair. Struggling, she got halfway up into an awkward, twisted position, then lost her balance and fell sprawling into the chair. Somehow, in the bucking and wiggling and tugging, the recliner popped open into its most extreme position. A loud *ripppp*. Her head jerked back; her feet flew up; her arms and elbows went every which way.

She batted the tattered gown from her face and fought with the recliner—which had transformed into an undulating octopus—to get to her feet. One ragged part of the hem still held her prisoner. Feeling as helpless as a staked goat, she kept struggling until she saw Flint enter with a black designer suitcase. She lay back, exhausted.

"I brought something for you." He opened the suitcase and dumped its contents into her lap.

She stilled. Her eyes widened.

Money. Banded stacks of bills. Dozens of stacks. *Scores* of stacks.

When she saw that most of the packets were in denominations of fifty and one hundred dollars, her eyes widened even further and she sucked in a deep gasp. "What is this?"

"A million dollars. It's yours."

"Mine?"

"Yep. I told you when I left that I would bring you back a million dollars."

"But you were teasing and that was *six* years ago."

"It took me a little longer than I expected."

"It's been *six* years, Flint. Six years without a word from you. Was I supposed to sit around and wait after you jilted me on our wedding day?"

"I didn't jilt you, sweetheart. I explained that I had a once-in-a-lifetime opportunity, one that might let me offer you a decent living instead of one with a river rat. I couldn't marry you and take you home to that shack my mother died in. I only asked you to wait, to give me a little time."

"A little time?" she shrieked, bounding to her feet amid ripping and rending noises. Fists on her hips, she glared up at him. "You expected me to wait for *six* years without a word from you? Without a phone call? Without a letter? Without a simple postcard?"

"I did try to call you, and I did write to you. And I damned well expected you to wait more than six *weeks* to marry another man! Was he rich?"

"No, Charles wasn't rich, but he...he was there when I needed him. He wasn't off gallivanting all over the country chasing a dream and trying to make his fortune. Why didn't you take me with you, Flint? Why didn't you take me with you?"

She watched pain and regret fill his black eyes. He reached to coil a lock of her hair around his finger. "I wish I had," he murmured. "I wish to hell I had."

The wrenching tone of his voice almost melted the steel armor protecting her heart, but she stiffened her resolve. "But you didn't. You made your choice and left me behind. Now it's too late."

"Is it, Julie? Is it too late for us?" He scooped up several stacks of bills, held them out to her and smiled that smile that had always turned her into mush. "You can have anything your heart desires. I've brought you a treasure."

Fury flew over her. She slapped the cash from his hand. "Keep your money! I never wanted money. I only wanted you." Despite her best efforts, tears ran down her cheeks.

"Oh, sweetheart," he said, gathering her into his arms, "I'm yours."

Before she could wiggle free, his mouth slanted over hers. Sensual, warm, familiar.

She melted under his sensuous spell. His lips evoked an avalanche of delicious memories that smothered her protests and plunged her into a sea of pure sensualism. His tongue branded her as his, only his.

Holding her close, he dropped kisses over her face, trailed his tongue along her jaw, nibbled on her earlobe. He cupped her buttocks, drew her against his hardness and groaned. "God, how I want you, darlin'. I've ached for you for six long years." His mouth devoured hers.

Reality crept through the cracks of her consciousness and dashed her with cold water. She tensed and tore her lips away. "What are you *doing?*"

"Gettin' me some sweet, sweet sugar," he murmured, reaching for her lips again.

"No!"

"No?"

"You heard me. I can't believe you're doing this. I'm engaged to another man. I should be married and at my wedding reception right this minute. You cannot kiss me. No."

"Babe, I wasn't the only one doing the kissing. You were going after it pretty good yourself."

"Don't call me babe. You know very well I've always hated being called babe."

"Sorry, darlin'."

"And don't call me darlin', either. I'm not your darlin'. I'm not your anything. I am about to become Mrs. Robert Allen Newly."

"*Newly?* Julie *Newly?*" A snort of laughter exploded from him.

She bopped him on the shoulder with her fist. "Don't you dare laugh. Yes, I'll be Julie Newly, and it's not funny. It has a lovely lilt. And if you know what's good for you, Flint Durham, you'll take me back to Travis Creek right this minute."

"Not until we talk."

"Why have you suddenly become so enamored with talking? Before you left here, all you did was grunt occasionally. You were certainly never a verbal communicator."

He shot her a salacious grin. "I was always better at the nonverbal stuff. You never complained about that."

Julie felt her cheeks heat. "I've matured."

"So have I. That's why I want to talk. We have a lot of things to straighten out."

Julie couldn't miss the stubborn set of his jaw. She knew from past experience that trying to convince him otherwise would be like trying to argue with a fence post. She would give him ten minutes, listen to what he had to say, then demand to be returned to her parents' house.

Still in a huff, she strode to a straight chair, plopped down and said, "Start talking."

Three

___

Flint dragged another straight chair to face Julie and straddled it backward. He crossed his arms over the top slat, rested his chin against them and stared at her, absorbing her image. How often he'd dreamed of seeing her again, ached for her. Now he felt like a desert-parched man at a crystal-clear oasis. He slaked his thirst on the loveliness of her face, a face that had first captivated him fifteen years before and had profoundly altered his life. Time had been gracious to her, drawn her beauty more keenly, transformed her from a lovely girl to an exquisite woman.

"You're more beautiful than ever," he said, speaking his thoughts aloud.

"Thank you," she said, her nose going up and her blue eyes turning frosty, "but you have exactly ten minutes to have your say. I would suggest that you use your time on topics more important than my looks."

He grinned at her imperious tone. "Right. Where shall I begin?"

"I'm sure I wouldn't know. You're the one who skipped town on our wedding day."

"Darlin', I didn't skip town. I explained that I wasn't ready to get married. All I had to my name was two hundred dollars in the bank, a shack on the water and a used Harley. I was earning barely enough as a fishing guide to support myself. I couldn't give you the things I wanted you to have or provide a decent place for you to live."

"You'd been telling me the same tale for *two* years. I was sick of waiting. I told you dozens of times that money wasn't that important to me. Besides, I had my teaching job. We could have gotten by just fine."

"But I didn't want to just get by. I wanted—" He scraped the red kerchief from his head, tossed it aside and raked his fingers through his hair. God, how to say this? "I wanted to give you fine things and a big beautiful house. But more than that, I wanted to be somebody, somebody that your family wouldn't look down their noses at. Somebody you could be proud to marry in front of the whole damned town instead of having to sneak off and find a justice of the peace. That's why, even though it took me eight years to do it, I got my college degree. I had a burning desire and a crazy idea that I could be a writer.''

Her brows went up and her eyes grew wide. ''A *writer? You?*''

''Yep.'' He rested his chin on his arms again. ''I've always had a powerful urge to write. In fact, I used to stay up half the night, pounding away on an old typewriter I scrounged up. I fancied myself as the next Ernest Hemingway.''

''This is the first I've heard of it. Why in the world didn't you tell me?''

''Pride, I guess. Nobody knew except Miss Fuller, my English teacher in high school, and Dr. Stephenson, my creative writing teacher at Lamar.''

Her eyes turned sad. ''I can't believe that you didn't tell me something so important to you.''

''I'm sorry. I should have, but I was waiting until I sold something. All I'd done was collect enough rejection letters to paper the whole courthouse. What kind of a profession was writing for somebody like me—the town bad boy, that old drunk Wilber Durham's kid? Hell, maybe I was deluding myself in thinking that I could be a writer. I was scared to death that you would laugh at me.''

''Gee, thanks! It's nice to know that you thought I was so shallow and insensitive. No wonder you jilted me!'' She sprang to her feet. ''This has gone far enough. Take me home this minute.''

''Not until I've had my say. Remember, I have the keys.''

She rolled her eyes upward and made exasperated growling sounds between her clenched teeth. She marched around in quick circles, pulling at her hair, most of which had come loose from its pins and hung in charming dishevelment. He knew that she was furious and getting madder by the minute, but he was desperate. No way in hell was he going to let her get away until he made her understand that the two of them were meant for each other.

"You have to sleep sometime," she said, smirking.

"Julie, honey, will you listen to me? I'm trying to explain. I didn't jilt you. I asked you to wait for another year."

"And after that it would have been another year... and another."

"I promised you that a year was all I was asking."

"You promised me that you would write to me, too, but you didn't."

"I did write to you. I wrote you several letters."

"Baloney! I never got them."

He frowned. "You didn't send them back to me with the newspaper clipping from your wedding?"

She looked truly stunned. "Certainly not."

"Then who did?"

"I don't know." Julie dropped to the chair, hung her head and was silent for several seconds. "My mother," she whispered. "It could only have been my mother." She looked up, a pained expression on her face. "Dear Lord, how could she have done such a thing when she knew—'' She clamped her mouth shut and glanced down at her fingers.

"When she knew what?"

Tears trickled down Julie's cheeks. "When she knew how...how much I loved you, how much I needed you."

Flint's heart nearly choked him. "Oh, darlin'." He pulled her up from her chair and into his arms. "I love you, too. And I need you. I hurt from needing you." He started to kiss her, but she started hissing and spitting like a wildcat. "Babe, what's wrong?"

"What's wrong?" she shrieked. "'What's *wrong?*' he asks. You waltz off to become Ernest Hemingway, then waltz back in six years later—on my wedding day, I might add—and expect me to take up where we left off? Well, think again, bub. And don't call me babe."

"But I explained, or at least part of it. If you had read my letters—"

"But I didn't read them."

He raked his hands through his hair again. "You would have if it hadn't been for that bitch of a mother of yours."

"Don't call my mother names!" she yelled.

"She's called me worse."

Julie jacked up her chin and glared lightning bolts. "She has not. She never even says 'darn.' But *I* have. I've called you every name in the book for leaving me. Would you like to hear some of them?" She let loose with a string of invectives that turned his ears red.

"Julie! I don't like to hear you talk like that."

She cocked one eyebrow. "Well, la-de-dah. Isn't that just too bad? If my choice of words offends you so badly, you can just take me home. Maybe I can still salvage my wedding."

"No chance. Cuss until you're blue in the face, but you're staying here until I make you understand that there will never be anybody else for you except me."

"You're going to have a long wait." She turned her back and crossed her arms.

"Honey, will you let me explain why I had to leave Travis Creek in such a hurry?"

"I'm not talking. I'm not listening." She covered her ears and started singing "Dixie" again.

"Dammit, Julie," he yelled. "I had received a letter the day before that knocked me for a loop. I was offered a full scholarship—"

"Look away...look awaaaaaay Dixieland," she caterwauled.

Exasperated, he retreated to the couch and sat down. He plunked his booted feet on the pine coffee table, picked up a magazine and began leafing through the pages. He couldn't have read it if he'd wanted to, not with all that howling and screeching going on. Julie was gorgeous; she had a well-modulated speaking voice that was sexy as hell; and he loved the woman with all his heart and soul—but the bare-faced truth was that she couldn't carry a tune in a bucket. Never could sing worth a damn. Six years hadn't changed that, either.

A few minutes later, she ran down. After an interval of blessed quiet, she said, "Flint, will you please take me home now?"

"Nope."

She sighed theatrically. "Well, if you won't take me home, at least let me go to the bathroom."

"Okay." He stood. "I'll take you."

"Home?"

"No. To the bathroom."

"I can go by myself. Where is it?"

"Outside."

Julie wrinkled her nose at the accommodations. At least it wasn't a little house down a path. The small room, which seemed to have been added as an afterthought to one end of the long back porch, had a shower, a toilet, a sink and...a window without bars.

But when she tried pulling it up she almost got a hernia. Examining it closely, she saw that the blasted thing was nailed shut. Oh, what she wouldn't give for a claw hammer or a pair of pliers.

Flint banged on the door. "Are you okay in there?"

Her keeper. She couldn't even go to the bathroom without him standing outside waiting for her. Some way, somehow, she had to escape from this place.

He banged again. "Julie, are you okay?"

Frustrated and furious, she flung open the door. "Can't I even use the ladies' room in peace?"

"Sorry." If she hadn't known better, she would have thought that he looked contrite.

Hiking up the tail of her torn wedding dress, she brushed past him, then stopped to scout the area, trying to figure out where she was. The cabin was in a heavily wooded tract, built partly on land and partly on beams over the edge of the bank. A pier extended out from the porch steps, but she didn't see a boat anywhere. All she saw was woods and lake—miles and miles of woods and lake. But there had to be a boat around somewhere.

Boats and water had always made her nervous, but because of the twins, she'd worked hard at overcoming her fears. She still wasn't thrilled about getting in a boat, but she could manage if it meant freedom.

Julie walked to the porch railing and nonchalantly glanced down at the water lapping at the beams. A red bass boat rode in a slip beneath the porch.

"Where are we?" she asked casually.

"At a friend's place on Lake Rayburn."

She shot him an exasperated glare. "I figured as much. But where exactly?"

He grinned. "Uh-uh. I'm not biting that line." He turned her to him. "Julie, don't even think about trying to sneak out and take off. Riding the Harley is out, and I know how you feel about boats and water, and you can't make it out on foot. If you tried, you'd only get lost and endanger yourself. We're a long way from anywhere." He stuck his fingers in his back pockets and sniffed the air. "Besides it's going to rain before long."

She glanced at the sky over the water. The sun was heading down—which at least gave her a directional clue—and a few clouds streaked its face, but the weather was clear as a bell. Before she could open her mouth to refute his claim, the wind kicked up a chill breeze, and she heard the rumble of distant thunder. Or was that her stomach? Clamping her hand on her tummy, she asked haughtily, "Are you going to starve me, too?"

He chuckled. "Hadn't planned to. Let's see what we can rustle up in the kitchen." He gestured for her to precede him into the cabin.

"You go ahead. I think I'll stay out here for a while."

He lifted one black eyebrow in a who-do-you-think-you're-kidding expression.

"Oh, all right!" She stomped indignantly inside—or as indignant a stomp as she could manage in her stocking feet.

If she was going to remain Flint's prisoner, be-damned if she was going to cook, and she told him so. While he fixed dinner, she tossed the trailing tail of her ragged dress over her arm and wandered around the cabin, looking for a way to escape. She checked every window and rattled every door. She surreptitiously scavenged through cupboards and drawers, trying to find something, anything, that might help her get away. Mostly she found fishing stuff: spools and spools of line, dozens of lures and other paraphernalia, and—*voilà!*—needle-nose pliers.

Glancing quickly over her shoulder to see if Flint had spotted her find, she stuffed the pliers down the front of her dress, adjusting them inside her bra so that they wouldn't make a telltale bulge.

Divine smells coming from the stove set her stomach to rumbling again—not surprising since she'd been too nervous to eat lunch, and breakfast had been a banana. She ignored the temptations Flint was concocting and continued her scrutiny of the cabin. With only two rooms and the kitchen alcove, she soon ran out of places to look. There were only so many spots to examine in such small quarters. Before she was reduced to anxious pacing, she told herself to calm down and think. Make a plan.

Picking up a stray stack of cash, she sat down on the sofa and fanned through the banded bunch of hundred dollar bills. Her eyes narrowed as she considered the money that he'd dumped in her lap earlier. The dozens of packets still littered the recliner and the floor.

Where had so much cash come from? Had he become involved in something sinister? Her mind conjured up all sorts of terrible scenarios. Had Flint gotten mixed up in... in drugs? Panicked, she swallowed. Oh, dear heavenly days, for all she knew, he was a dope fiend or a bank robber. Or maybe—

"Julie!"

She yelped and jumped two feet off the couch. "Don't creep up on me like that."

"I didn't creep. I called you twice. Dinner's ready."

"Oh. Uh, uh, I need to wash my hands in the bath-room."

"Wash them at the kitchen sink."

She patted her disheveled hair. "Well, I'd also like to straighten up a bit. Do you have a brush?"

"Sure, in the bedroom on the dresser. I'll pour the wine."

So much for her idea of working on those window nails in the bathroom. When Flint turned his back, she made a face, then snatched up a stack of bills and hurried to the bedroom. The cash might come in handy. She stuck the packet of money in her garter, the blue one that she should have been tossing to pro-spective grooms about now. Her family must be wild with distress. She only hoped that they didn't alarm the children.

When she saw her reflection in the mirror, she didn't even care that she was a mess. Her lipstick was gone, and her mascara was runny and smeared. The circlet of roses and the attached veil had been blown off in the wild ride. Only one limp rose dangled at her tem-ple. She plucked it from her hair and tossed it aside. After removing the pins, she gave her tangled mop a good brushing, then ripped a strip from her dress and tied the scrap around the hair she gathered at the nape of her neck.

She tried to do something with her mascara, but her efforts only made matters worse. Lips pursed, she marched back into the kitchen area and announced,

"Flint, I look like a raccoon. I need to wash my face in the bathroom where I can see what I'm doing."

He grinned. "Okay. Come on. But hurry up. Our dinner will get cold."

After he escorted her to the bathroom on the porch, Julie cleaned the mascara streaks in thirty seconds. Leaving the water running, she yanked the pliers from her bosom and went to work on the nails. She had one nail out and another loose when Flint knocked on the door.

"Come on, sugar. Our dinner's getting cold."

She muttered a curse. "Just a minute," she called. She pulled out the second nail and quickly stuck the pliers beneath a plunger in the corner. She turned off the water, turned on a smile and opened the door. "I'm ready."

Inside, the table was set, a candle was lit and soft music played on a radio. He held her chair as she sat down.

Worry about her predicament should have taken away her appetite. It didn't. She was famished. And common sense told her that if she was going to escape, she needed to keep up her strength. Besides, the food was delicious. Beyond delicious.

Fish sautéed in mushrooms and herbs, pasta in a delicately seasoned cream sauce, cold asparagus marinated in olive oil and balsamic vinegar with sun-dried tomatoes. And the wine was fabulous.

"Enjoying your dinner?" he asked.

She looked up from shoveling in a mouthful of pasta. He toyed with the stem of his wineglass while he watched her. Amusement played around the corners of his mouth. Embarrassed to have been caught stuffing food in her mouth like a starving refugee, she put down her fork and delicately dabbed her lips with her napkin.

"It's quite tasty. Where did you learn to cook like this?"

"In California."

"I see."

"Want to know what I was doing in California?"

"Not particularly." She chugalugged the rest of her wine. He filled her glass again.

"Thank you."

"You're welcome."

She nodded toward his untouched fork and picked up her own. "Aren't you going to eat?"

"I'd rather watch you."

"Well, don't," she said, lifting a bite of fish to her mouth. "It makes me nervous."

"It makes me horny."

Her fork clattered to her plate. "Damn you, Flint Durham, don't say things like that to me."

"Would you want me to lie?" His voice was barely a whisper.

His eyes, smoldering like a banked camp fire, bored into hers. A tendril of raw sensual awareness traveled between them and stroked her skin. Quivering sensation rippled over her. She tried to glance away, but she was helplessly mesmerized by the potent allure of his dark eyes. Black with longing, they seemed to draw her into their depths, mesmerize her with memories of a passionate past.

A low throb began building in her body, quickening her pulse and stealing her breath. Knowing that she was flirting with disaster didn't stifle the feelings. The forbidden enticement seemed only to fan the flames. The attraction was still there, stronger than ever, as if it had been secretly intensifying beneath the surface for six long years. She struggled, waging an inner battle between desire and dignity.

Abruptly, Julie sprang to her feet. Her chair overturned and crashed to the floor. "Don't do that!" she shouted.

"Don't do what, darlin'?"

"Don't look at me that way."

One corner of his mouth lifted in a lazy smile. "What way is that?"

"As if . . . as if I were dessert."

His smile broadened. "You want dessert?"

"No. I've had quite enough! I want to go home. Now." She had to get away from him. She *had* to. Six years' worth of barriers erected from bitterness and disillusionment were beginning to crack. She wouldn't let that happen.

"Sorry, babe. Not yet. Not until we talk, really talk."

"I have nothing more to say to you. I want to brush my teeth. Do you happen to have an extra toothbrush?"

"I think there's one in the bathroom."

Spine stiffened, she walked to the rear door and waited until Flint unlocked it.

As soon as she was in the bathroom, she turned on the water and grabbed the pliers. With strength born of desperation, she yanked out the three remaining nails in the window. Her heart hammering like crazy, she tugged it upward. It stuck briefly, then slid open. She blew out a relieved breath. Standing on the toilet, she hitched up her torn dress and threw one leg over the windowsill.

"Julie!"

She froze.

Flint rapped on the door. "Julie, are you okay in there?"

"Dammit, Flint! Would you at least allow me some privacy? I'll be out in a minute."

"Sorry," he mumbled, sounding contrite.

She poked her head out the window and surveyed her surroundings. In the gathering dusk, the lake was still. The woods were hushed. The ground beneath the window was only a few feet down. Maneuvering herself through the opening, she held on to the sill, then dropped.

She landed ankle deep in muck.

Oh, gross. She stilled, listening for a second, then scrambled up the bank.

Sharp stones and stickers shredded her stockings and punished her tender feet. Shoes. She had to have shoes. Wincing with every step, she hurried to the spot where her silk pumps were still stuck heel deep in the ground. She grabbed them up and, dancing on first one foot, then the other, stuck them on her muddy feet.

Hoping against hope that Flint had left the key in the Harley, she ran to the motorcycle. No such luck. Panicked urgency growing, she hesitated, her darting eyes scanning the densely wooded area, trying to decide which way to go, what to do next. She couldn't try for the boat; it was moored just beneath Flint's feet. After spotting an outbuilding through the trees, she dashed toward it, praying that it held transportation.

She flung open the door and almost wept with joy. A pickup truck!

Her joy was short-lived. No key.

Panic increased, clawed at her insides until she thought that she would scream.

Wait!

In the corner.

A bicycle.

It wasn't in the best shape—in fact, it was in pretty sorry shape—but it would do. She pushed it to the door and, after peering around the opening, pushed it outside. The frame was a little bent, and the back tire was almost flat, but it was transportation.

A streak of lightning flashed. She heard Flint bellow her name just before a boom of thunder rolled through the trees. The wind picked up, whipping branches and snatching at leaves, ballooning her skirt. Batting at the billowing silk, then gathering her tattered hem into a wad, Julie gritted her teeth and climbed on the bicycle.

She didn't look back. She didn't dare. She picked a likely direction and started pedaling the wobbly bike as fast as her legs would churn.

Four

Pedaling in high heels was murder, and no matter how much she wrestled with it, the tail of Julie's bedraggled wedding dress kept getting caught in the spokes. She hadn't gone a quarter of a mile, and already she was exhausted from trying to make headway on the decrepit bike. Only stubborn determination kept her herding the rickety thing down the lane in the fast-fading light. At best, she had only a half hour before dark. She had to get home to her babies, who were sure to be upset and frightened, and to her family, who was bound to be frantic by now. And to Rob, of course.

Another boom of thunder struck, reverberating through the dense woods. The wind plucked at the yards of material tucked around her. She slapped away flapping fabric as the air grew chill and the tops of tall trees swished and swayed. When the first big splats of rain hit, she groaned. *Oh, no. Please, no.*

The tempo of the pelting raindrops increased. The sky darkened until she could barely see where she was going, and the drops rapidly escalated until they became a hard downpour.

Behind her a motor roared to life.

Her heart caught.

She pedaled faster, but as the dirt road turned to mud, the going got tougher. She could hear the engine of the Harley coming closer and see the headlight cutting through the torrent.

The rain plastered her hair to her head, rivulets of water ran off her chin, and her dress had turned into a sodden anchor when Flint pulled aside.

"What in the hell do you think you're doing?" he yelled over the howl of the storm.

"I'm going home," she yelled back, never taking her eyes off the road.

"You can't get home on that thing and in this storm. You're going to break your fool neck. Come get on with me, and let's get out of the rain."

"Stick it in your ear, Flint Durham! I'm going home."

Julie pumped the pedals with everything she had; but she wasn't gaining much ground. The bike grew more and more wobbly, and she had to fight to keep it straight. Her arms and legs quivered from the strain.

She knew that she couldn't go on much longer, but she'd rather eat liver than admit it to Flint.

Suddenly she hit a hole. The jolt snatched the handlebars from her grip. The bicycle went one way; she went another. With a teeth-jarring splat, she belly flopped into a puddle. She spat, sputtered and cursed, then rolled over onto her back. As she lay spread-eagle in the middle of the oozing mud, she squinted at the sky and conceded defeat to the evil rain god that pummeled her. Dejected, disgusted, she closed her eyes and let the weather do its worst. She couldn't get any more soaked, and she was too damned exhausted to care.

Flint went sick all over when he saw Julie lying there drenched to the skin and still as a corpse. Furious with himself and scared out of his mind, he jumped off the bike, knelt beside her and began running his hands over her body, checking for injuries. "Babe, oh, babe, open your eyes. Darlin', are you hurt?"

She opened her right eye and glared at him. "Only my dignity. Get your hands off me. And don't call me *babe!*"

"I won't, sugar." He continued checking for injuries until she slapped his hands away. Ignoring her protests, he scooped her up and started to the Harley.

"What do you think you're doing?" she demanded, struggling in his arms.

"I'm going to take you back to the cabin and get you out of the rain and out of those wet clothes."

"No! I'm not going." She started bucking like a wild bronco. "Put me down."

"Dammit, Julie, be sensible! I'm not going to let you strike out alone at night and in a thunderstorm. We're going back to the cabin. You can do it the easy way or the hard way. Either calm down and get on the Harley behind me, or I'll walk back and carry you over my shoulder like a sack of potatoes. Which is it going to be?"

It seemed like forever before she stopped struggling, grew quiet, then meekly said, "I guess I have no choice."

The tone of her voice was so pitiful that it cramped his heart. If he hadn't loved her so much, he would have put her on the back of the bike and taken her home right then. But he did love her. He was fighting for his life, his future—their future. He clenched his jaw and said gruffly, "That's right. No choice."

He got on the motorcycle, and she dejectedly joined him. As he headed back to the cabin, he could feel her exhaustion as she leaned against his back, and he felt lower than worm dirt when he felt her shivering and heard her teeth chattering.

As soon as they returned, he jumped off the bike, gathered her into his arms and strode up the steps and through the house. He didn't stop until he reached the bathroom. There he set her on her feet and unzipped the back of her muddy, sodden wedding dress.

"What are you *doing?*" she shrieked, batting at his hands.

"I'm going to get those wet, filthy clothes off and get you into a warm shower before you catch pneumonia."

"Like hell you are!"

"Like hell I'm not!" One yank and the dress plopped to the floor. She was left in a lacy bra, panties and stockings held up by blue ruffled garters. A packet of hundreds was stuffed into one garter. "What's this?" His thumb riffled the bills.

Her chin went up. "Mad money." She yanked the money from her garter, slapped the stack against his chest and shoved. "Now would you get out and let me take a shower?" Her teeth were still chattering. She clamped them together and jacked up her chin another notch.

He tried to maintain a stern expression, but he could feel a smile coming on. Standing there like a drowned cat but still as feisty and proud as a lioness, she was so precious, so adorable. God, how he loved her. He wanted to take her in his arms and never let her go again. And standing so close, seeing her rosy nipples hard against the transparent lace of her bra, stirred and flashed heat through him. His jeans tightened.

He wanted her. Bad. Fighting the impulse, he dragged his eyes from her breasts and met her gaze. He almost groaned aloud. *Get a grip, Durham,* he told himself.

To her he said sternly, "I'm not leaving you alone in this bathroom."

"But—but—" she sputtered.

"The point is not negotiable."

Slicing him with a look designed to make him bleed, she turned in a huff and stepped into the shower. She yanked the curtain with such force that it overshot its mark, and she had to yank the other end back in place.

One muddy shoe flew from the cubicle. Then another. Two blue garters, lacy and ruffled. A pair of once-white stockings, shredded and stained, sailed out.

Flint grinned and waited for the rest. None came. The water went on, and steam began to billow over the curtain. He gathered up her ruined clothes, rolled them into a bundle and tied them securely with her stockings. First chance he had, he was going to burn the whole mess. The only wedding dress he ever wanted to see Julie in was the one she would wear when she married him.

He opened the door wide enough to toss the bundle onto the porch. When he turned around, Julie's wet head was poked out of the curtain.

"May I have towels, please?"

"Sure." He retrieved a stack from beneath the sink and tossed her a couple.

In a few minutes, she slid open the curtain and stepped out, a blue towel wound around her body and a green striped one wrapped turban style on her head. If her chin had been jacked up any higher, she would have gotten a crick in her neck.

Without a word he ushered her back to the bedroom. He grabbed a pair of dry jeans and underwear from the bureau drawer.

"Feel free to put on anything you can find. I need a shower myself." He started to leave, then turned back. "Don't even think of trying to leave again. I'm locking the doors, and I have the keys to all the transportation. When I get back, we're going to talk."

Wearing oversize gray sweats that had seen better days, Julie sat huddled on the couch. She'd finally conceded that she couldn't wear her own clammy underwear, and the baggy outfit did more to hide the fact than a pair of Flint's jeans and a T-shirt. She couldn't find any shoes that came close to staying on her feet, so she settled for a pair of thick tube socks.

Working on damp wet hair with Flint's brush, she noticed that logs and kindling were set in the fireplace. A warm blaze would be just the thing to ward off the chill and help dry her hair.

She found a box of matches and was about to strike one when the back door opened. She glanced over her shoulder and almost swallowed her tongue.

Flint came in toweling his long dark hair. He wore only a pair of low-riding jeans, zipped but not buttoned. Julie tried to strike the match, but so rapt was her attention to his bare chest that she missed the emery strip completely. She remembered that chest well. Her fingers had once memorized every smooth muscle and corded tendon, every swirl of soft dark hair.

Her lips had often followed the trail from his belly button to that enticing spot where his jeans gaped—

She jerked her gaze upward until her eyes met his, dark and intense. Heat flushed up her neck.

"Julie," he murmured. "Oh, love."

He stepped toward her, but she quickly turned away and fumbled with the match, trying to strike it against the box. The match broke. She cursed, threw it down and fumbled for another. She tried striking it, but her hands were shaking so badly that she made a mess of it.

"Here, honey," he said, taking the box, "let me."

The match flared on his first try. Kneeling, he held the flame to the kindling. Julie's gaze slid over his back where the light caught droplets of water and set them glistening against the broad expanse of tanned muscle. How her fingers ached to touch that familiar smooth skin, to trace the old scar on his shoulder and to feel the corded strength of the contours.

As the kindling sizzled and flared, she felt a similar sensation deep within her, a flame flickering and licking at old memories, growing hot, gaining strength, ready to burst into full blaze.

Her chest went tight.

No! she told herself.

Her breasts began to swell.

No, no! I can't remember. It's over.

Her womb started to throb.

She tried to move, but she couldn't. A host of long-restrained emotions struggled at their bonds, threatening to break free and engulf her. From the moment that she had first seen Flint Durham, he had captivated her. From the moment that their eyes had met in the library the summer that she was sixteen, she had known that there would never be anybody else for her. Never.

Only Flint could make her heart sing; only Flint could make her soul soar. Some dark magic in his eyes could steal her reason and release mindless, searing passions so intense that it was frightening. Remembering that intensity, she sucked in a shuddering breath.

Her whole body vibrated. She dared not look into his eyes now.

Please, please, don't let him turn around.

As if he heard her thoughts, he turned, looked up at her and smiled.

Elemental awareness sparked between them, hissing and spitting like the logs in the fireplace. He stood. His brow wrinkled as if he were in pain, and his eyes swept over her like a bittersweet caress. Then, without uttering a word, he held out his arms to her.

With a soft cry, she moved into the circle of his arms, into the flame. His lips met hers and ignited an inferno. They both went wild—licking, tasting, thrusting fiery tongues. Ablaze, their bodies writhed. Their hands stroked and moved frantically—hers, over the corded muscles of his shoulders, his back, through his long damp hair; his, over the curves of her body and under the sweatshirt to stroke her bare skin.

With a guttural groan, he quickly pulled the shirt over her head, then lifted her so that her breasts were accessible to his mouth. At the first flick of his tongue against her nipple, she went up in flames. She wound her legs around his waist, threw back her head and keened a soul-deep cry.

As Flint continued to lave and sip and taste, he murmured familiar love words against her heated skin. Each murmur, each touch, fanned the flames higher until she wept from desire.

"Tell me what you want," he whispered.

"You. Only you."

With her legs still wound around his waist, he strode to the bedroom.

Five

I'm paralyzed! were Julie's first panicked thoughts. She felt as if she were bound with steel cables. Her eyes popped open. She gave a sigh of relief when she realized that the steel cables were only Flint's arm and leg flung over her, holding her spoon fashion against him. His breath was warm against the crown of her head.

Flint?

Ohdearlord! She was in bed with Flint. In *bed.*

Naked.

And she . . . and they . . .

They hadn't.

Ohdearlord. They had.

Twice.

Or was it three times?

A sick feeling squeezed her throat, then slid down her esophagus and landed like a ten-ton boulder in the pit of her stomach. She couldn't believe what she had done. She'd just spent her wedding night with another man.

What had possessed her to do such a thing?

She knew the answer to that one. Flint Durham had possessed her. As strong a person as she was, one smoldering look from his dark eyes, and she'd gone up like a gasoline-soaked bonfire. She couldn't even blame her idiocy on too much wine. She'd been stone cold sober.

The charisma Flint exuded was her weakness. Always had been. When he left, he'd carried a part of her with him, the best part, she sometimes thought. It had taken a long time to get over him, to be able to endure the endless painful days alone, to be able to sleep through the night without dreaming of him, but, by damn, she had. She'd pasted the shattered pieces of her ego together and gone on with her life. She had relegated all memories of Flint Durham to the far reaches of hell.

Now, in less than twenty-four hours, he'd turned her well-ordered life into chaos. She had betrayed her fiancé, embarrassed her family and corrupted her own values. All for a roll in the hay. She had put a sack over her brain and given in to raging hormones. How could she have been so spineless and shallow? So incredibly stupid?

Self-loathing engulfed her.

She had to get out of there.

Slowly, she eased from the weight of Flint's arm and leg, grateful that he was a sound sleeper, and slid from beneath the covers. Shivering from the chill of the dim predawn morning, she gathered up the gray sweatpants and socks, then tiptoed into the other room for the shirt.

As she pulled on the clothes, she tried to think of how she could get away. The truck in the garage was the best bet. The keys should be in his pants.

She tiptoed back into the bedroom. A board creaked under her foot. It sounded like a ten-car pileup. She froze, her heart beating like the timpani section of the Boston Pops.

Flint snuffled, groaned and turned over.

When he quieted, she started breathing again. It wouldn't do for him to wake up anytime soon. She wanted a big head start.

A malevolent idea popped into her head.

A diabolical smile lifted one corner of Julie's mouth as she surveyed her work. She'd used every roll of fishing line she could find in the cabin. Oblivious to his state, Flint lay sleeping peacefully in a cocoon of nylon cord that passed over him and under the bed. When he woke up, it would take him forever to get loose from the web she'd wound.

She quietly opened the chest and took out another pair of socks. Keys in hand, she crept from the room and closed the door. She donned the second pair of socks and pulled on Flint's boots. They were miles too big and sloshed on her feet when she walked, but they would do.

After checking to make sure all the doors and windows were locked, she took a bill from the money packets still scattered on the floor and stuffed it into the side of the boot she wore—for an emergency. She locked the front door behind her.

The storm had moved through, and the weather had cleared, but lingering dampness hung heavy in the early-morning air, magnifying the scents of pine, oak and sweet-gum trees and the wet humus beneath them. As she eased down the steps, she spied the Harley under the lean-to off one end of the cabin and briefly considered disabling the motorcycle. Her first impulse was to forget the Harley and hightail it out of there, pronto. But Flint was a clever man, extraordinarily resourceful and never one to be underestimated.

She didn't know exactly the best way to disable the bike, but whatever she did, it had to be quick and thorough. Rapidly considering and discarding ideas, she settled on filling the gas tank with handfuls of pebbles and mud.

"That ought to do it," she said with a smug bobble of her head. She wiped her muddy hands on her pants as she ran for the truck.

Flint Durham wasn't the only one who was clever. If he'd been around for the past six years, he would have known just how resourceful *she* had become.

She'd bet that suitcase full of cash that he'd never underestimate her again.

Julie got lost twice, but she finally found her way home about the time that the town was beginning to rouse. A few cars were already parked at the Baptist church for early service, and the Sunday paper was in the driveway when she pulled to a stop.

The big white house looked still, quite ordinary really. She didn't know what she was expecting exactly, but she had pictured a tearful reunion with her family waiting anxiously on the lawn for her return.

Nobody waited for her on the lawn—if you didn't count Poochie, Mrs. Menefee's beagle, who was marking the new camellia bush at the corner of the porch. Even Poochie gave her only a brief glance before he turned and trotted away.

She sat in the truck a long time, trying to think of what to say to her family. To Rob. She'd been searching for the right words all the way home. Still, she didn't have a clue as to what to say. What could she say?

What had been everyone's reaction the day before when Flint had pulled that outrageous stunt? And what had been happening since she'd been gone? She wanted to find out a few things before she walked into the lion's den. Actually, she was chicken. She wasn't ready to face the questions, the censuring looks, just yet.

Her hand shook as she cranked up the truck. She drove only a half block away and stopped in front of a big Victorian house with fading pastel blue paint and a thick drapery of wisteria vines screening one end of the porch. The thicket of vines formed a cozy retreat that concealed a swing suspended by a chain and an assortment of wicker tables and chairs. She could almost smell the gingerbread baking as she went up the walk. This was the safe haven of her childhood.

Grandma Travis's house. She'd spent many hours curled up next to Grandma on the swing.

But Grandma Travis had been dead for eleven years, and her grandfather had died long before she was born. Uncle William lived there now. Actually, he'd never left home except for the few years he'd spent at Harvard. Of all her sons, William, her youngest, was most like Beatrice Travis—except for the inordinate amount of bourbon and branch water he consumed—warm, gentle, accepting and very, very wise.

The chain on the porch swing creaked softly as she climbed the front steps. Uncle William marked the book of poetry he was reading—his favorite Keats, Julie noticed—and smiled as he rose. His clothes were only slightly rumpled, and his eyes were only slightly bloodshot. A gentleman of the old school, his rangy good looks and retiring manner had always reminded her of a cross between Ashley Wilkes and a young Jimmy Stewart.

The reason for his drinking was a family secret that Julie and Melissa had never been privy to, but from snippets she'd pieced together from various sources, she gathered that some woman from Boston had broken his heart about the time he got his law degree. As a teenager, she'd thought the notion very romantic.

Now she thought his alcoholism very sad. As a young man he'd practiced law halfheartedly and had served two terms as county judge. These days he went to his office only occasionally to draw up a deed or a will. Such a waste of a brilliant mind.

"Good morning, my sweet Juliette," he said in the sonorous voice of a born orator. "Would you like some coffee?"

"Please."

He poured from a heated silver pot into a fragile china cup that was from her grandmother's favorite set. She took the cup and settled into the soft depths of a cushioned wicker chair. Uncle William added a dollop from a silver flask to his own cup and returned to his position on the swing.

For several moments, they didn't speak. They simply sipped their coffee and inhaled the peace of the retreat where traces of Grandma's loving spirit seemed to permeate the walls, the furniture and the leaves of the wisteria coils.

Julie set her cup aside and hugged her knees to her chest. "That was quite a scene at the altar yesterday, wasn't it?"

William cleared his throat. "I'll have to say that yours was the most...interesting wedding that I've attended in some years." Amusement tinged his words.

"Did everybody have a hissy fit?"

"That seems an apt description for the behavior I noted—after the initial shock subsided, of course. Everyone was running around like ants after their bed is stirred. Except your mother. She conveniently fainted."

Julie buried her face in her hands and groaned.

"Don't despair, my sweet. A bit of stirring up is what the lot of them needed. I thought the whole thing was phenomenal. When John Durham came roaring in like the hand of God on that big black Harley, I almost stood up and cheered. In fact, I believe I did cheer." Uncle William and one or two teachers were the only people who ever called Flint by his real name. Uncle William hated nicknames.

"Cheer?" she asked, surprised by his comment. "For heaven's sake, why?"

"Because, as you know, I never thought that Robert Newly was the right man for you. What now? Are you still going through with your marriage to the young butt doctor?"

"Uncle William!" she chastised.

"Sorry, dear. I couldn't resist. Someone with your fire is wasted on Newly. You need a man who can appreciate your passion, knows how to stir it to life and harness it. A man like the one who braved the whole town to spirit you away yesterday. Is the old spark still there? Do you still love him?"

"I don't know. Oh, Uncle William, I'm so confused." When tears started trickling down her cheeks, her uncle held open his arms to her, and she joined him on the swing. While he offered his handkerchief and patted and soothed her, she spilled the entire story of what had transpired from the time of her abduction.

When her tale was finished, she sat up and blew her nose. "Mercy, what a mess! I hate the idea of having to face everybody. I can't marry Rob—at least, not until I do some strong soul-searching—and Mother will make my life miserable. What am I going to do?"

"Where does John fit into this?"

"Nowhere. He blew his chance six years ago."

William started to comment, then checked himself. After a moment, he said, "What would you really like to do right now?"

"Right now?" She gave a hollow half laugh. "I'd like to take the kids and run away from home so that I wouldn't have to listen to everybody unload on me. I'd like to go someplace secluded and peaceful and just kick back and forget about this whole horrible mess."

"Sounds like a fine idea to me."

"Are you serious?"

"I am. Take the twins on a vacation. Get away from your parents and Travis Creek. You need some time to yourself."

She sighed. "I wish I could. Where would I go? I can't see staying in a hotel with Megan and Jason. They would be bored and miserable."

"Hmm. I might have an idea. I know someone who has a house in a remote part of California. He's not using it at the moment, and I believe it comes with horses and a swimming pool. How does that sound?"

"Like the answer to a prayer."

"You go home and get packed. I'll see if I can have things arranged by this afternoon."

A few minutes later Julie eased in through the sun room door, which was rarely kept locked, pulled off Flint's oversize boots and went looking for her family. Following the smell of coffee to the kitchen, she found only the dregs of an old pot still warming. She checked the den and stopped abruptly when she spotted Melissa and Rob.

Melissa wore a pink robe, and Rob wore the pants of his tux and a wrinkled white shirt with the sleeves rolled up. They were both on the couch, sound asleep. Melissa's head rested on Rob's chest, and his arms were around her. Coffee cups and plates with the remnants of dried sandwiches littered the table.

A sharp pain of shame pierced Julie as she stood in the doorway and watched them.

For the first time she realized that one part of her had been glad when Flint had interrupted her wedding. She'd had a few niggling doubts about marrying Rob, but she had refused to consider them. Now she knew that there was no way she could marry Rob—not after what had happened. He was too nice a man. He deserved a wife who loved him deeply and fiercely, with all her heart and soul.

Melissa stirred and opened her eyes. When she spotted Julie, she squealed, "You're back!"

Rob woke with a start. "Julie! My God, we've been frantic." He rushed to her and gathered her into his arms. "Are you all right?"

"I'm fine," she said, her face crushed against his shirtfront. "How are the twins?"

"Sound asleep," Melissa said. "Finally. They loved all the excitement."

"Was it awful?" Julie asked.

Melissa sighed. "Pretty bad. Uncle Hiram put out an APB, and the place was swarming with police. Why, I don't know, since you were long gone from here."

"Exactly where have you been?" Rob asked quietly.

"I'm not sure," Julie told him. "It was a remote cabin on the lake."

"What happened?" His tone had the hint of an edge to it. "Did that bastard harm you in any way?"

Julie shook her head. "Not really. He just wanted to talk to me. He's . . . he's . . ."

"I know who he is. Melissa told me."

Julie felt her heart drop to her toes. She hadn't told Rob who the children's real father was. She'd planned to a dozen times—right up to the time of the wedding—but the time never seemed right. Now she had another reason to feel guilty.

Melissa looked frantic and was making copious facial gyrations out of Rob's sight. "I told him that Flint was an old boyfriend that you'd ditched years and years ago—even before you married Charles. I told him not to worry, that Flint wouldn't hurt you. Everybody knows that while Flint was always a little wild, he was basically harmless. Isn't that right?"

"Right. Melissa, would you excuse Rob and me for a few minutes?"

"Oh, sure. I'll go tell the folks that you're back. No, cancel that. Dad's blood pressure went sky-high, and Mom developed a raging migraine. Dr. Hastings doped them both up and sent them to bed. I think I'll go take a shower instead. Are we going to reschedule the wedding? Jason's furious that he didn't get to do his part, and the flowers are still fresh. Of course Mom—"

"Melissa, *please,*" Julie interrupted.

"Oops. Sorry. I'm gone." She hurried from the room.

Julie sighed and turned to face the music...Rob.

When he tried to gather her into his arms, she gave him a brief hug and gently eased from his grasp. "Rob, I'm sorry for the spectacle that Flint Durham caused. I'm sure that it was painful for you and that your family and friends were as mortified as mine were."

"Honey, the important thing is that you're back safe and sound. Under the circumstances, I suppose that the formal wedding is off, but there's time for us to have a quiet ceremony and still make our flight to London this evening."

She shook her head, then tried to speak around the lump in her throat. "I—I think that we'd better cancel the wedding altogether, Rob."

He looked stricken. "Cancel it?" His eyes narrowed and bored into hers. Feeling guilty as sin, she had to look away. "What happened at that cabin, Julie?"

She opened her mouth, but nothing came out. Dear God, she couldn't tell him the truth.

"Did he . . . did he rape you?"

She shook her head violently. "No, no. Nothing like that. He didn't hurt me. It's just that...I've had some time to think, and . . . I've decided that I'm not ready for marriage right now."

"You picked a hell of a time to decide that!"

Julie winced at his anger. "Rob, I'm sorry. So sorry."

Looking crestfallen, Rob touched her cheek. "Don't you love me?"

Her heart almost broke. Why couldn't she feel fire and passion for this man? Why didn't her soul soar when he was near? Why didn't her senses go wild when he touched her? He would make the ideal husband. The ideal father. Rob Newly was perfect. Perfect.

But the chemistry just wasn't there. She couldn't pretend any longer.

"Of course I love you, Rob. You're the sweetest man alive. I . . . I just don't know—"

He laughed and hugged her to him. "Of course you love me, and I love you. You're merely upset about this bizarre episode, and it's giving you the jitters. Natural. Absolutely natural. We'll have the minister perform the ceremony immediately after church services, and we can be off to London. Why, in no time, we'll be laughing about this."

Gently disengaging herself from his arms, Julie said, "No, Rob. Marrying you now would be a big mistake. I was about to say that while I love you, I don't know if I'm *in* love with you. There's a difference."

The laughter had left his eyes. "Is it him?"

"Who?"

"That long-haired bastard on the motorcycle. Is he the reason for this?"

"No. *I'm* the reason. I'm a mixed-up mess. I'm sorry, Rob. So sorry." Tears welling in her eyes, she turned and fled.

Six

When Julie spotted the small dark-haired man who stood shyly to one side of the baggage area, she could have kissed him. The hand-lettered sign had her name on it. With stops, the flight from Houston to Palm Springs had taken five and a half hours, and by the time they landed, the twins' novelty and excitement of a plane ride had worn thin. They had grown restless and a little cross from the confinement.

Julie released Jason's small hand to wave to the man, and the little boy was off like a shot. She resisted the urge to shriek at the child, knowing that he needed to run off some of his pent-up energy. "Megan, would you catch your brother and bring him back? Don't either of you dare go outside without me."

"Yes, ma'am," Megan said, running after Jason.

Julie looked heavenward and sighed, thankful that the airport was small and that they were unlikely to get lost.

As the man with the sign approached her, he whipped off his cowboy hat. "Señora Julie Stevens?"

"Yes."

He broke into a broad smile that crinkled the deep squint lines around his eyes. "I am Javier. I drive you to Señor Juan's home."

"Oh, thank goodness. I don't think I'm up to renting a car and driving in a strange place. The kids and I are pooped, and I have a tendency to get lost. Jason takes after me. That's why I sent Megan after him. She has a built-in homing device."

Javier's smile died as she spoke. He looked puzzled. "*¿Como, señora?*"

She laughed. "Never mind me. I tend to babble when I'm tired. Where did those children go?" She craned her neck looking for them.

"*¿Los niños?*"

"Oh, dear. You don't speak English? Uh, *¿habla usted inglés?*"

His vocabulary was limited, but with his little bit of English, her rusty high school Spanish and sign language, they managed to communicate well enough so that Javier went to collect the luggage while Julie went in search of Jason and Megan. She found them in the gift shop with noses pressed against a glass case. Jason was enthralled with a collection of rubber hunting knives, and Megan was gazing wistfully at a stuffed kitten with soft white fur.

Feeling guilty about dragging them away from their playroom full of toys, Julie allowed them to make one purchase each, and she picked up a local travel guide and a couple of paperback novels that looked interesting.

Soon they and their big pile of luggage were loaded into a Jeep Cherokee and were driving along a crowded one-way street, headed south. Beyond the town were stark foothills that served as reminders that this green valley had been carved from desert. Driving through Rancho Mirage and Palm Desert, they passed fabulous homes and luxurious desert resorts that boasted lush lawns, flower beds and the inevitable palm trees. She'd heard of the area, of course, but she'd never been to this part of California.

Uncle William had promised that, except for a couple who handled the chores, she and the twins would have his friend's house to themselves for as long as they wanted.

Nervous that Flint would escape his bonds and come after her, she had gathered belongings quickly, tossed their bags in the car, and Melissa had driven them to a hotel near the Houston airport. Neither Melissa nor her parents knew her destination. In fact, Julie hadn't known exactly where she was going until the tickets were delivered to her hotel room. Uncle William had taken care of everything.

"Where is our house?" Jason asked from the back seat. "Are we almost there?"

"I don't know, sweetheart," Julie said. Uncle William had said that the house was in a remote spot, but frankly, the notion of being stuck in a desert didn't exactly thrill her. As an East Texas girl, she preferred trees and lakes over cactus and sand. In halting Spanish, she asked Javier about their destination as he turned off the main drive onto a winding road.

"*Allá*, there," Javier said, pointing. "Over Santa Rosa."

"Over the mountain?"

"*Sí*, over the mountain."

The road began to climb steeply, dramatically, with a series of switchbacks and curves. Julie checked the travel guide she'd bought, trying to figure out where they were.

"Wow!" Jason said. "Look at that! We're going really high."

"Is this where Heidi lives, Mom?" Megan asked.

Julie laughed. "No. We're in California. Heidi lived in Switzerland, in the Alps."

As the Jeep climbed toward the summit of the mountain, she understood why the guidebook described their route as the Palms to Pines Highway. The palm trees and desert plants began to give way to pine trees and junipers and other verdant vegetation as the geological features changed.

After about half an hour of twisting upward, they came to the summit and began to descend. Julie's breath caught at the beauty of what she saw below. There, in an area only a few minutes from the desert, shone a lush valley of green meadows and thick pine groves. They passed a large lake and several small dirt roads that cut off the main highway.

Javier turned onto one of the dirt roads that wound through a wooded tract. At its end was a large house made of split logs weathered to a honey gold. A long veranda stretched across the front and baskets of red flowers hung along its length. A smaller house was off to one side and a barn and other outbuildings were off to the other.

Behind a fence two bays and a beautiful palomino mare cropped the lush meadow grass.

"Oh, Mom, look! Horses!" Jason shouted.

"Horses!" Megan squealed, as well. "Oh, Mommy, may we ride the horses? I've always wanted to ride a horse. I like the blond one."

Javier laughed as he pulled the Cherokee to a stop near the front door. "Those too big for you, *niños.*"

"No, they're not," Jason protested. Megan agreed, promising that they would be *very* careful.

"Sorry, kids," Julie said. "Those are fine animals, but they're far too much for you to handle."

Megan's bottom lip went out, and Jason began to mumble under his breath.

"*Mañana* the ponies come," Javier said as he began unloading the luggage.

The pouting and grumbling stopped abruptly. "Ponies?" The twins spilled out of the car and surrounded Javier.

"*Sí.* Ponies. Little horses." He measured waist high with his hand. "*El patrón,* he send the ponies and saddles for the *niños.*"

"Wow! Can we ride them?" Jason asked, dancing from one foot to the other.

Javier glanced at Julie and raised his eyebrows, waiting for her response.

Megan tugged at Julie's hand. "Oh, Mommy, please, please, please, please. We'll be very, *very* good, won't we, Jason?"

"Very good. Eggsimplewary."

Megan rolled her eyes. "*Exemplary.* That means exceptionally well behaved."

Julie burst into laughter. "Exemplary? Exceptionally well behaved? Where did you hear that?"

"From Dr. Rob," Megan said. "He said that if our behavior was exemplary while you were on your honeymoon we could have a dog. I told him that I'd rather have a kitten. Mommy, are you and Dr. Rob ever going on a honeymoon? I really, *really* want a kitty. A white one, like this." She held up the stuffed animal she'd bought at the airport. "But I want a real one."

"I'd rather have a dog, but they can't go on a honeymoon, silly," Jason piped up. "They're disengaged. Aren't you and Dr. Rob disengaged, Mom?"

Julie struggled to keep a straight face. "Yes, I suppose you could say that."

Jason made a face at Megan. "See, I told you. You can't have a cat, 'cause Gran is 'lergic."

"She's 'lergic to dogs, too. And who would want an old dog, anyhow? They pee on the carpet, Rosie said."

"Not if you teach 'em to pee outside. And cats pee, too."

"Only in a littler box. They're fast—fast— They're very, *very* neat. Mommy, why aren't we going to marry Dr. Rob and go live with him? I really, *really* want a kitty."

"And I want a dog. A big one. Maybe a German shepherd. I'd take good care of him. I'd feed him and water him and take him outside to pee, honest to Pete I would, Mom."

"I understand," Julie said, ruffling Jason's unruly dark hair and squeezing Megan's hand gently. She sat down on the porch steps and pulled the twins close. "But I thought I explained last night that Dr. Rob and I aren't going to get married. Are you two very unhappy about that?"

Megan sighed. "No. I guess not. He wasn't a real daddy, anyhow." She snuggled closer to Julie. "I don't think he liked me and Jason. Is that why you didn't go on the honeymoon?"

"No, sweetheart. It had nothing to do with you two. It was other things—grown-up things. And I think Dr. Rob liked both of you a lot. He just doesn't have much experience with children."

"I'm glad we didn't marry Dr. Rob," Jason said, "but Melissa was real sad about it. Yesterday before he left, I saw her kissing and kissing him. On the *mouth*. Yuck! Then she went to her room and cried and cried. I heard her through the door. You know who I wish was my daddy? The Black Knight!''

Julie frowned. "The Black Knight?"

"Yeah. The Black Knight on the motorcycle who stole you from the wedding. He was cool!"

Megan rolled her eyes. "The Black Knight can't be our daddy, silly."

Jason glared at his sister. "Why not?"

"Because he has long black hair and tattoos all over his body! His kind is nothing but trash, Grandpa said. He's mean and scary and smells bad."

"Does not!"

"Does, too!"

Not quite sure how to deal with the twins' argument over Flint, she was grateful to be saved by the appearance of a plump Mexican woman who was as ebullient as Javier was shy. Introducing herself as Alma, Javier's wife, she clucked over the twins and drew them all to her ample bosom in welcome, then shooed them inside to get settled.

Julie loved the house immediately. Off the foyer was a large room decorated in a comfortable southwestern style with a huge fireplace. There was also a large dining room and a kitchen to the other side. An additional wing belonged to *el patrón*, Alma explained in English no better than Javier's.

Javier carried the bags upstairs to the guest rooms, which were off a small sitting area. Like the downstairs, the decor was colorful, casual and comfortable, not like the pristine formality of the Travis home. Julie's room had its own bath and the twins had rooms that flanked another bath. Every room had a beautiful view—of pine groves or meadows or mountains in the distance or of the pool and flower beds near the house.

Alma, who the kids took to immediately, scooted the pair to their rooms to unpack, promising cookies and milk in the kitchen when they were done.

Julie wandered out onto a balcony off her room and leaned against the railing, drinking in the essence of the place. The sky was an incredible blue, the grass an unbelievable green. She breathed in deeply, savoring the fresh crispness of pine-scented air, and as she breathed out, she felt the tautness that knotted her neck and shoulders relax its grip and flow from her body. She hadn't realized how tense she was.

Again she took a deep breath and let it go. This wasn't merely tension from the past two days, she realized. Nor was it a result of the turmoil of wedding plans. Those knots had been there a long, long time.

She had desperately needed this. Uncle William had been a wizard to find such a perfect, peaceful place.

Julie turned the palomino mare into the pasture and smiled as she watched Jason and Megan brush the ponies after their ride. She hadn't been on a horse in years, as her protesting muscles had reminded her for a couple of days. But after the kinks were worked out, she loved being in the saddle again, and the children took to riding like ducks to water. The past week had made a definite change in the twins. While they had always seemed happy and well adjusted, she couldn't remember when she had heard them laugh so much. And they were busy from dawn till dusk, exploring, riding the ponies, swimming, helping Alma bake cookies or trailing after Javier asking endless questions. They were even picking up a little Spanish.

"I'm going up to the house to take a shower and read for a while," Julie told the kids. "Have you finished with Rusty and Daisy?"

"All done," Megan said, leading her spotted pony into her stall.

"Me, too," Jason said, putting Rusty away. "I want to go swimming." He tore off for the house, but Julie grabbed the waistband of his jeans as he ran by.

"Whoa, pardner. You can't go in until later. Remember our rules. There must be an adult around."

"But Javier—"

"Javier has gone into town, and Alma can't swim, remember?"

"Oh, yeah." He kicked a rock with the toe of his boot. "Shoot."

"Alma said we could help her bake a chocolate cake and lick the bowl," Megan reminded him.

"Awright!"

They were off like a pair of bottle rockets.

Julie walked more sedately to the house. As she approached, she glanced at the empty downstairs wing and wondered again about the owner of the home she'd come to love. Curiosity had sent her exploring on her third day there, but the door to the owner's suite had been locked. Embarrassed as she was to admit it, she'd even tried to peek in the windows. But the drapes were drawn, and she couldn't see a thing.

Ordinarily, she wouldn't have been so curious, but sometimes late at night, after Javier and Alma were in their cottage and the children were asleep upstairs, she sat alone in the soft leather chair in the great room. Somehow she knew that it was his chair. A lingering masculine essence seemed to permeate the leather and palpate the air around her.

She would curl up in the chair's comforting depths and fantasize about the man who had built this house and selected the furniture, the paintings, the books on the shelves. Everything there spoke of strength—not a harsh brawn, but a steady, determined strength that you could count on. Power tempered with gentleness.

As Julie passed through the great room, she paused by the chair to stroke her fingers along the supple leather. What did he look like? she wondered. Neither Alma nor Javier could be coaxed into saying much about their employer. In fact, the pair's understanding of English became even poorer when she asked. She didn't even know her host's last name. She did learn that he was unmarried and had something to do with the film industry. Was he a famous movie star who fiercely guarded his privacy?

Surely not. How in the world would Uncle William know a movie star?

On the other hand, Uncle William did get around a lot. He knew a surprising range of people all across the country.

Whoever he was, the potent traces of her host's personality seemed infused into the very walls, and their presence sparked and titillated feelings deep inside her. Sometimes she had an intense, almost overwhelming urge to pick the lock to his room and fling herself into his bed. She imagined herself wallowing restlessly in a tangle of sheets, his hot breath on her neck . . .

"Come off it," she murmured aloud, then laughed at herself. She couldn't believe that she had allowed her daydreams to become so rash. Making love with Flint Durham had been a mistake in more ways than she had realized. Since then, her libido had turned recalcitrant, and here she was getting all revved up over a figment of her imagination.

Her host was probably twice her age and gay.

Upstairs, Julie stripped off her horsey clothes and got in the shower. She didn't need a man complicating her life. Not *any* man. Not some fantasy man she'd conjured up, not Rob Newly and certainly not Flint Durham, damn his black eyes!

It was time that she learned to take care of herself and her children without depending on anyone else. The twins would be starting kindergarten in the fall. Before then, she would find a teaching job—some-

where other than Travis Creek, and away from her
parents—and buy a small house. Maybe she'd even get
a place with some acreage so that the kids could have
a couple of ponies. With the trust fund from her
grandmother and her salary, she could swing it.

Yes, she thought as she reached for a towel, that was
exactly what she was going to do.

The shriek of children's laughter jerked Julie awake.
She heard more squeals and giggles. Splashing water.

Splashing water?

She jolted upright, and her book fell to the floor.
Were the children in the pool? Was Javier already
home? Had she dozed that long? She checked her
watch. He wasn't due back for hours.

If those kids were in the pool without adult super-
vision, they were in for it!

Bolting up from her chair, she stalked across the
room and flung open the doors to the balcony. "Megan! Jason!"

Megan squealed with laughter as she shot up from
the water, hoisted on the shoulders of a dark-haired
man, who roared like a grizzly as he rose from the
depths. With Megan straddling his neck and clutching his long wet hair, the man turned.

"Hi, Mommy," Megan shouted, grinning and
waving broadly. "Look who's here."

"The Black Knight!" Jason yelled.

"Flint Durham! What in the name of heaven are you doing here?"

A slow smile spread across his face as he looked up at her. "Just playing troll."

Seven

"Uh-oh," Jason said as he hung on to the side of the pool beside Flint. "Now you're in for it."

"Think so?" Flint asked.

"That was Mommy's angry voice," Megan said from his other side. "She only uses it when something is really, *really* serious."

"Yep. It always means that we're gonna get punished. But don't worry. She won't hurt you. Mom doesn't sock us or beat us with a belt or nothin' like that."

"No," Megan added. "Mommy says hitting little kids is child abuse. Mostly she just talks to us and sends us out on the back porch to sit. Sometimes we lose privileges, like watching TV or riding our bikes or playing with our friends.''

''I see,'' Flint said, fighting the urge to smile. Julie had a pair of cute kids. Except for her dark eyes, the little girl was a miniature Julie. Jason, with his dark hair and eyes, must take after his father.

His father.

Dammit! Flint burned with envy for a dead man. He hadn't even known about the children until a few days ago when William Travis had driven out to the cabin and cut him loose. Julie's uncle had been Flint's patron more than once.

''Yep,'' Jason said. ''When I hear Mom's really angry voice, it's always big trouble. Like if I let my dog pee on the carpet.''

''Jason Stevens, you don't even have a dog!''

''Yes, I do. He's a German shepherd, and his name is Rex.''

Megan made shaming noises. ''Jason, you're telling a story. You do not have a dog. Gran is 'lergic.''

The back door slammed. ''Uh-oh, here comes Mom.''

Flint watched Julie charge to the pool like an avenging angel. With fists on her hips, she glared down at him. He cringed from the poison darts her eyes shot. Before she said anything, he put an arm around each twin. ''You wouldn't hit me in front of the children, would you?''

Megan cupped her hand over her mouth and giggled. ''Mommy doesn't *hit,* silly. I told you that.''

"I may make an exception in this case," Julie said around clenched teeth. "Jason, Megan, go inside and get dressed. I want to speak to this man alone, please."

Flint boosted the pair onto the apron. With water streaming from her pigtails and her tiny pink bathing suit, Megan tugged at her mother's hand and said in a loud whisper, "Mommy, he doesn't smell bad, and he doesn't have any tattoos. I looked. He's very nice."

"Yeah," Jason whispered, just as indiscreetly. "I like Flint. He's cool. Don't be mad at him, Mom."

As Julie looked down at her son, Flint saw her face soften. She brushed his wet hair from his forehead. "You two get your towels and run along now. Be sure to squeeze out your suits and hang them up."

"Yes, ma'am."

"Yes, ma'am."

Flint smiled as the twins scampered away. "Great kids."

"Thank you."

"They're good little swimmers. I'm surprised."

"Why?"

"Because you were always so scared of water."

"Things change. In six years, lots of things change."

"And some things stay the same." He hoisted himself from the water and stood. "Like the sparks we strike."

He wanted her so badly that he could have taken her right then. Stripped those little shorts down her long legs and laid her on the picnic table. All week his body had ached from the frustration of loving her and wanting her.

Julie stepped back. "Stay away from me, Flint."

He lifted his hands in a gesture of innocence. "I haven't touched you."

Her eyes narrowed. "I can read your mind. It isn't difficult. How did you find me?"

"It wasn't hard. If you have the right connections and spread a little cash around, you can find out almost anything."

"Very well. You've found me. Now you just turn around and go right back where you came from."

He picked up a towel thrown over the back of a chair and rubbed it briskly over his head and wiped his face. Catching the towel at each end, he looped it around Julie's neck and pulled her to him. "Can't."

"Why not?"

Capturing her gaze with an intense one of his own, he slowly lowered his mouth toward hers.

"Don't," she said, her voice soft and husky.

He stopped half an inch from her mouth. She didn't move, but he heard her breath catch. He was so close that he grew hard just from the sweet scent of her.

"I want you to leave," she said, still not moving away.

"Liar." The tip of his tongue slowly traced the seam of her lips. Back and forth. Slowly. Back and forth. He felt her mouth tremble.

For the longest time, she didn't budge. Then suddenly she jerked at the towel and shoved him away.

"Don't do this to me, Flint," she said, her words a desperate plea. "Leave me alone." She wheeled and fled into the house.

"No way, babe. No way. Not this time."

He wasn't exactly sure how he was going to do it, but he planned to marry Julie before she hooked up with somebody else again. It was a miracle that he made it to Travis Creek in time to stop her from marrying that wimpy proctologist. If William hadn't by chance noticed his name on the credits of his latest film and contacted his agent—God, he didn't even like to think about it.

The kitchen door opened, and Alma came bustling out with a tray in her hands. "Señor Juan, you want some lemonade?"

"Thanks, Alma." He picked up a glass and gulped down the drink. "That was great. You make the best lemonade in the world. Why don't we ditch Javier and you and me get married?"

She laughed at the familiar joke. "Oh, *señor*, you *loco*." She leaned close and whispered, "I like your Señora Julie. A very nice lady. *Muy bonita*. And the little ones, oh, they are a joy."

"Can you keep our secret a little longer? I don't want Julie or the kids to know that this is my house just yet."

Alma looked bewildered. "But why not? This is a beautiful house, Señor Juan."

"I know, but trust me, it's best that she not know for a while. She would take the kids and leave, pronto.

And another thing, try to remember to call me Flint, not John or Juan.''

"Flint?" She looked even more bewildered.

"Yes. Flint Durham. And please remind Javier when he returns. It's very important. Okay?"

She shrugged her shoulders and rolled her eyes as a comment on his peculiar requests. "Okay."

"And I'm going to tell her that you invited me to stay."

"*Me*, Señor Jua—Señor Flint?"

"Yes. Just play along, Alma. Please."

As she left he could hear her muttering in Spanish all the way to the house.

Still shaking all over, Julie leaned back against her closed bedroom door. Just when she thought she was recovering from her last encounter with Flint, here he came again. She hadn't recovered at all. Being around him had always turned her emotions chaotic. She had wanted to drown him in the pool when she'd first spied him with the children, but when she had looked into her son's dark beseeching eyes, her anger had evaporated.

Jason's eyes, Jason's expression, were an exact replica of his father's. Of Flint's. Megan had his eyes, as well, but Jason looked like a five-year-old version of his father. Flint must be blind not to have noticed the striking resemblance between them.

Or had he?

Surely not.

Oh, dear Lord, what was she going to do? The twins longed for a daddy like other children had, but they had accepted that their father, Charles Stevens, had been killed in an automobile accident when they were too young to remember. But Charles Stevens was a fictional character. Flint Durham was their father, and he was here.

Did the twins have a right to know that Flint was their father?

Did Flint have a right to know that the twins were his children?

How would she know if Flint could be a decent father? She knew nothing about his life for the past six years except that he'd learned to cook sophisticated dishes and had a suitcase full of cash—which, for all she knew, he'd made dealing cocaine.

Julie began to pace, heartsick and torn about the situation, trying to decide what to do. Flint's desertion six years ago had cut deeply; nothing in her life had ever hurt her more than that. Finding herself abandoned and pregnant had thrown her into the yawning black pit of a depression so awful and so profound that she'd seriously considered suicide to escape the horrible pain. For endless weeks and interminable months she hadn't cared whether she lived or died. Every one of those wretched days was Flint Durham's fault.

She didn't trust him. She didn't think that she could ever trust him again. Her first instinct was to protect herself and her children by packing them up and running fast and far.

But that hadn't worked the last time.

And she was an innately fair person. Perhaps Flint and the children deserved some time together. Even if they didn't know their true relationship.

And she wasn't about to tell them. Not yet. She wasn't that crazy.

Around and around her thoughts chased. When she went downstairs to dinner two hours later, she was still in a quandary. Maybe she was getting all riled up for nothing. Maybe Flint had heeded her pleas and left. Maybe seeing that she had two children had scared him off.

And maybe the Pacific Ocean was banana pudding.

Wearing jeans and a T-shirt, his long hair tied at his nape with a leather thong, Flint sat in the middle of the floor playing Sorry! with the twins. If Megan had gotten any closer to him, she would have been sitting in his lap, and Jason was watching his every move with blatant hero-worship.

Flint looked up from the game and smiled that bone-melting smile. Why had God given him such a potent weapon? The sexy heat of it went directly from his mouth to her heart—*thunk,* like an Olympic javelin.

He stood, stuck his hands in his back pockets and cranked the smile into a killer grin. "Hello, there. We were about to send a posse out for you. Those smells from the kitchen were making us mighty hungry."

Jason stood and stuck his hands in his back pockets. "Yep, mighty hungry."

"It's Alma's pot roast they smell," said Megan, pressing herself against Flint's leg. "And Flint smells good, too. He said it's from a little something he picked up on Row-day-o Drive. That's in Los Angeles, California. He has a 'partment there. But he used to live in Travis Creek a long time ago. Like us. Did you know that?"

"Yes." Julie cleared her throat. "Yes, I did." To Flint she said, "I thought that you would be gone by now."

"Oh, no. I plan to stay with you and the kids for a few days. Alma said that it wouldn't be a problem."

"She was mistaken. I'm sorry, but I'm afraid that we don't have a room for you," Julie said sweetly, trying to be polite in front of the children.

"He can stay in my room with me," Jason piped up. "He can have the top bunk."

"Yeah," Flint said, grinning smugly. "I can have the top bunk in Jason's room."

"I don't think you'd be comfortable there."

"Oh, sure I would. Don't worry about it—I'm adaptable. What say, kids, are you ready for dinner?"

"Yeah!"

"Yeah!"

"Come on, sweetheart. Let's eat." Flint took Julie's arm, tucked it in the crook of his and swept her, sputtering protests and all, into the dining room.

After dinner Flint had envisioned a crackling fire, a bottle of wine and Julie snuggled beside him on the couch. Instead, Julie had retreated to her room to read and left him downstairs with the kids. He sat on the couch, Megan on one side and Jason on the other and both in pajamas, and watched a movie on the Disney channel.

Some romantic evening. How was he going to convince Julie to marry him if they never spent any time together?

By ten o'clock that night, Flint was good and miserable. Jason had been sound asleep since nine-thirty, but Flint lay scrunched on the top bunk in Jason's room, wishing to hell that he was in his king-size water bed downstairs. Bunk beds were never designed for adults of his height.

By eleven he was even more miserable. How could he sleep, knowing that Julie was in bed less than a foot away? Only a wall separated them, but it might as well have been a continent. Still, his body responded as if she'd been in his arms.

Restless, he turned again, trying desperately to find a comfortable way to rest without his shorts strangling him. He usually slept in the buff, but as a concession to modesty around the kids, he'd worn a pair of boxer shorts to bed. Hell, he didn't even own a pair of pajamas. Now he knew why.

At midnight he was still awake, staring at the shadows cast by the night-light onto the ceiling. There wasn't all that much room between him and the ceiling. And the truth was that Flint was just a little claustrophobic.

Only for Julie would he endure this. Only for Julie.

A bloodcurdling scream shot Flint upright in bed. His head bashed the ceiling, and he cursed.

Another terrified scream blasted adrenaline through his veins and set his heart hammering. Still half-asleep, he flung the covers aside and jumped out of bed. Nothing solid met his feet. He plunged to the floor, landing in a bone-jarring sprawl. He cursed again. Profanely.

When another scream split the air, he scrabbled toward the source, careering off a wall and whacking his elbow. Dazed, he ran bull-like through the bathroom to Megan's room. Just as he yanked the door open, the door from the hall opened and Julie flipped on the light.

"My God, what's wrong with her?" Flint asked, panicked by what he saw.

Wild-eyed, Megan continued to scream as she tried to climb the wall behind her bed. Julie ran to the child and grabbed her by the shoulders.

"Megan, wake up," Julie said, shaking her gently. "Wake up, honey."

Megan, her eyes wide and glassy, continued to flail her arms and scream bloody murder. Julie seemed very blasé about the episode. Was she nuts? The kid was in agony.

"I'll call an ambulance," Flint said. "No, no. We can get her to the hospital quicker in the Jeep. I'll drive her. You carry the car." He reached for Megan.

Julie held the little girl away from him. "Calm down, Flint. This looks scarier than it is. I'll take her to the bathroom, and you wet a washcloth with cold water."

In the bathroom, Flint grabbed a handful of washcloths, tossed them in the sink and turned on the cold water full force. The bowl filled. Higher and higher went the water until it began dribbling over the rim.

He cursed and tried to turn off the faucet. He tried first one, then the other, and the damned things wouldn't stop. Water spilled over the counter and sloshed on the floor.

"Good heavens, Flint! What are you doing?" Julie sat the whimpering child on the counter and quickly shut off the water. She wrung out a cloth and began bathing Megan's face and talking to her.

"What's wrong with her?" he asked, still alarmed.

"*Pavor nocturnus.*"

"What?"

"It's commonly called night terrors."

He felt the panic rush from his body. "Oh, God. You mean she was only having a nightmare?"

She shook her head. "Not a nightmare. Nightmares are bad dreams. This is different. Night terrors occur during the deepest stage of sleep, not during the REM period when dreams happen. It's a developmental sleep disorder. She'll grow out of it eventually."

"You mean this happens all the time?"

"No. Only occasionally. She used to have episodes more frequently when she was younger. She hasn't had one in about six months. Megan, sweetheart, wake up. It's Mommy."

"But she's awake," he said. "Look at her. Her eyes are wide open." He bent and stared at the whimpering, shivering child. The terrified look in her eyes tore a hunk from his heart.

"Trust me," Julie said. "She's still asleep. Megan," she said to the little girl, "wake up." She swabbed her face with the cold cloth and shook her gently.

Megan grew still. Then she blinked and looked from one adult to the other, a perplexed expression on her face. "Mommy, why are we all in the bathroom?" She wiggled on the countertop, then glanced down and patted her thigh. "Mommy, I'm all wet." She cut her eyes quickly to Flint, then back to Julie and whispered, "I didn't... you know?"

Julie smiled. "No, pumpkin. You had a night terror, and Flint got a little exuberant with wetting a washcloth."

She giggled. "You made a *big* mess."

"I know. I'll clean it up. But you about scared me out of my drawers."

She glanced at his boxers. "But I didn't." She cupped her hand over her mouth and giggled again. "Mommy, look. He has lipstick kisses all over his shorts."

Julie rolled her eyes and gave him a withering look.

"Somebody gave them to me for a joke, okay?"

"I'll bet."

"We'll discuss this later. Is Megan all right?"

"See for yourself. She's fine. Right, baby?"

"Mom-my! I'm *not* a baby. I'm five years old."

"So you are. Let's get on some dry pajamas and go back to sleep." She lifted the child and set her on her feet. "I'm sorry that we disturbed you," Julie said to him.

"No problem."

When she turned and walked away, he noticed for the first time that she wore only a sheer nightgown. Every curve was visible as she stood in the light. His body jumped to immediate attention, and he had to stifle a groan.

Or maybe he hadn't stifled it. She whirled around, glared at him, then strode to the door and slammed it in his face.

Eight

As Flint climbed into Gazer's saddle, he winced.

Julie, astride Contessa, the palomino, frowned. "You look a little pale. Are you sure that you're okay?"

He resettled his cowboy hat and shot her a big smile. "Great, just great. How about you?" He sucked in a deep breath. "Smell that fresh air. It's a perfect morning for a picnic."

Flint had decided that he must have pulled something when he fell from the bunk the night before. His back and his hip had been giving him a fit all morning. Only with serious effort was he able to walk without a limp. He had promised the twins the night before that he would take them riding along a mountain trail for a picnic, and Julie had reluctantly agreed to go with them. He would have sooner swallowed roofing nails than to admit that he was in pain.

A good night's rest in a decent bed might have helped some, but he'd had neither rest nor a decent bed. He defied any adult to sleep folded up in that torture chamber he'd been stuck in. He'd dozed off for a few minutes a time or two, then woke up with a godawful crick in his neck.

Maybe he'd gone soft over the past few years. He could remember when he could sleep soundly in the fork of a tree.

"Ready, kids?" he called to the twins.

"Ready!"

"Ready!"

"Head 'em up and move 'em out." Flint took the lead as they started across the pasture to the foothills.

They rode slowly, taking time to look at an eagle's nest, a rabbit and clumps of small wildflowers. The twins asked a million questions, and he patiently answered each one.

After being in the saddle for a while, his back and hip didn't seem to bother him as much anymore. Just needed to work the kinks out, he figured.

When they had ridden for about an hour, much of the journey up a winding, well-defined path, he stopped in a clearing.

"How about this place for our picnic?" he asked the kids.

"Super. Let's eat."

"Yeah. I'm hungry."

"Julie?"

"It seems like a good spot." She dismounted, tied the palomino's reins to a bush and turned to help the children.

When Flint started to climb down off Gazer, the damnedest thing happened. His right leg wouldn't work. How in the devil was he going to get off the horse if he couldn't move his leg?

Clamping his jaw teeth tightly, he tried it again. Nothing.

Beads of sweat popped out on his forehead. *Now if this wasn't hell to pay.* He was too embarrassed to ask Julie for help. Or maybe too proud. Reaching back, he untied the bags that held their lunch and held them out to Julie. "I'll be right back," he told her.

She looked puzzled, but he kicked Gazer's sides and rode off before she could question him.

A short distance away, he found what he was looking for—a low, sturdy tree branch. Maneuvering the horse until he was positioned, Flint grabbed the branch and pulled himself from the saddle. When he lowered himself to the ground, his legs started to buckle. Cursing, he grabbed the saddle horn.

After some more cursing and some stomping and massaging, he legs started working again. But he was as stiff as a bois d'arc post and hurt like bloody rip. Grabbing Gazer's reins, he limped back toward the clearing.

When he neared the spot where Julie was spreading their lunch, he affected a rolling gait to cover his limp. "Howdy, there, pilgrims," he drawled in his best John Wayne imitation. "The grub about ready?"

Julie looked at him as if he'd grown another head, and Megan giggled.

Jason said, "Alma sent fried chicken for us. Which piece do you like?"

"I'm not choosy, pardner. You and the ladies can take your pick." He leaned against a pine tree, and watched Julie and the kids dish the meal onto paper plates.

Megan patted a place beside her on the blanket and fluttered her eyelashes at Flint. "You can sit here."

He grinned, wishing that Megan's mama was half as interested in flirting with him as her daughter was. "Thanks, sweetheart, but my setter is about worn out." He rubbed his rear end. "I think I'll stand for a while." Flint knew that if he sat Indian style on the ground, he wouldn't be able to get up before the first snows began.

Megan giggled, then carried a full plate to Flint.

Jason rubbed his bottom and said, "My setter is worn out too."

The boy picked up his plate and went to lean against the tree beside Flint. But Jason wasn't as adept at eating with one hand as Flint was. A good part of his food landed on the ground instead of in his mouth.

"Careful there, son. You're leaving most of your lunch for Old Two Toes," he told the boy.

"Who's Old Two Toes?"

"A bear."

"Are there *bears* around here?"

"Only Old Two Toes from what I hear tell."

"Why is he called Two Toes?" Megan asked from her position on the blanket.

Flint launched into a story about an old mountain bear, making it up as he went along. The bear, named by the local Indians, had been caught in so many traps that he only had two toes left on each paw.

The children were enthralled by the story, and the wider their eyes got, the more Flint added to the tale. He finally ended by saying, "Legend has it that, when the moon is full, if anybody can sneak up on Old Two Toes and touch his tail, that person's wish will be granted.

"Wow," Jason whispered, his face filled with awe. "*Any* wish?"

"That's what they say. But I'm not sure I'd want to find out."

"Why not?"

"Because Two Toes would eat you all up, silly," Megan chimed in.

"Okay, kids, no more talk of bears, or you'll be having nightmares," Julie said, clapping her hands. "Let's get things cleaned up."

"Sorry," Flint said to Julie. "I didn't mean to scare them. I'd hate to have a repeat of last night."

"The *pavor nocturnus*, you mean?"

He nodded.

"Bear stories don't cause the night terrors. As I told you, it's a developmental sleep disorder. The doctors have assured me that lots of kids have them in one form or another. Tooth-grinding, bed-wetting, sleep-walking and -talking, along with night terrors, are all stage-four sleep disorders. They often run in families, and they're usually outgrown sooner or later. True, stress sometimes makes them worse, but basically they're a biological or neurological problem."

"Come to think of it," he said, "I believe I used to walk in my sleep when I was a kid. Mama used to lock my door, afraid I'd walk into the lake and drown."

"But you never did."

"Nope." Flint gathered Gazer's reins. He prayed he would be able to mount without help. "Excuse me for a minute, would you?"

Julie watched Flint carefully as they rode back down the trail. He had acted strangely when they left. He seemed stilted, pale. Was he ill? Something was wrong. Since he led the way, she couldn't see his face, but his back was ramrod straight and his free hand was curled into a fist on his thigh.

When they reached the meadow, she nudged Contessa into picking up her pace and drew alongside Flint. She noticed that his face dripped with sweat and his shirt was soaked. It couldn't have been from the heat. Although the day was sunny, the temperature wasn't more than seventy or seventy-five.

"Flint?"

He didn't acknowledge her. His eyes stared straight ahead, and his lips were drawn into a fine line.

Alarmed, she called his name again. "What's wrong?"

"Nothing," he retorted.

"Don't lie to me! What's wrong?"

"Pain." He paled even more, his eyes rolled back and slowly he began to slide from his horse.

Julie jumped from the palomino, but she reached him only in time to partly break his fall.

"Jason! Ride and get Javier. Be careful, but hurry. Tell him to bring the Jeep."

Things were hazy for a while, but as Flint drifted in and out, he remembered Julie's sobs and her calling his name over and over as she kissed his face.

He smiled and stroked her fair hair as she leaned over him. "Shh, darlin'. I'm okay." He brought her fingers to his lips and kissed them.

"Glad to hear that, babycakes," a deep voice said. The fingers chucked his cheek. "Does this mean we're going steady?"

Flint's eyes flew open. He blinked the face into focus. "Kyle, what in the hell are you doing here?"

"It's my clinic. I have a right to be here."

Flint looked around and realized that he was on a table in an examining room. "Then what am I doing here?"

"Well, I was getting ready to do a nifty little facial peel on a director's wife, who shall remain nameless, when Javier, Alma, a gorgeous blonde, and two kids ran in screaming that you were dying. I abandoned the director's wife, who is going to be angry if I'm away much longer, and rushed out to save you."

"To save me?"

"I thought it was at least a heart attack, but your heart's in better shape than mine is. Want to tell me where it hurts?"

Flint pointed to the painful areas on his back and hip, and he explained about falling out of the bunk and having to sleep like a contortionist.

Kyle poked and prodded, and Flint jerked and winced.

"Hmm," Kyle said, then poked some more. "I think you pulled something, buddy."

"Hell, I could have told you that!"

"Hey, don't get testy. I'm a plastic surgeon—this is out of my field." He pressed a couple of other places and Flint almost came off the table. "Ahh."

"What 'ahh'?"

"Muscle spasms. Those I know about. You're knotted up worse than a backlash on a trout line. I'm going to shoot you with some potent muscle relaxant and give you some pills to take. Go home and stretch out in that big water bed of yours. I'll come over tonight and check on you if you'll ask Alma to bake me a lemon pie. Why in the devil were you sleeping in a bunk last night, anyhow?"

"It's a long story."

Dr. Kyle Rutledge smiled that boyish smile that reeled in women by the droves and had earned him a spot on every list of California's most eligible bachelors. "Could it have anything to do with the lovely lady pacing in my waiting room?"

"Hands off, pretty boy," Flint said to his friend. "This one is special, and she's all mine. Don't bother to come over tonight. I'll have Javier drive me here tomorrow."

"Uh-uh. When I said go to bed, I meant it. Stay flat for twenty-four hours. I'll see you tonight. My nurse will shoot you with joy juice and give you the pills. I have to get back to my patient."

Kyle was about to leave when Flint stopped him. "Uh, buddy, I don't know how to say this, but . . . I have a favor to ask. Could you pretend that you don't know me?"

The doctor raised one pale brow. "The director's wife can wait a few more minutes. This I've got to hear."

Despite her temptation to play Florence Nightingale, Julie didn't set foot in the master bedroom suite where Flint was situated. Alma and Javier insisted on taking care of the ailing interloper, and she let them. Alma seemed in her element, plumping pillows and carrying food trays.

Julie also kept the twins out of his room so that he could rest. That was no small feat. Jason and Megan already adored him, and that fact caused her endless consternation. She knew that the longer Flint stayed, the stronger the bonds between the children and him would grow.

As soon as he was physically able, she would ask him to leave. No, she would insist that he leave. After all, one of the reasons that she was here was to distance herself from Flint and the riotous emotions he stirred in her. How could she ever get her life together and make plans with him lurking about?

When Dr. Rutledge dropped in the second evening as well, Julie was surprised. "I didn't realize that doctors made house calls anymore."

Wearing a cowboy hat and boots with his jeans and denim jacket, the handsome blond doctor, who turned out to be a transplanted Texan, too, looked more like a rancher or a country singer than a surgeon. He smiled as he tossed his hat aside. "I'm just being neighborly. I live across the highway from the clinic, and...the owner of this house and I have been friends since I moved up here three years ago to get away from the L.A. scene."

As they walked to the open door of the master suite, she said, "Garner Valley seems like a strange place for a plastic surgery clinic. It's so remote."

"Since I opted out of the rat race, I deliberately keep my practice small. And actually, my patients enjoy the remoteness. They prefer someplace quiet and private like the lodge to recover. The clinic is fully equipped and staffed, and I have a helicopter and pad for emergencies that might require specialized care."

"And the scenery is beautiful."

He looked deeply into her eyes and smiled. "Very beautiful." His suggestive tone made it obvious that he wasn't referring to the area's sylvan view. "Perhaps we can enjoy the full moon together later after I—"

"Doctor!" Flint roared. "Get in here!"

"My, our patient is getting cranky, isn't he?" Dr. Rutledge said, amusement playing at the corners of his mouth. "We'll talk later over a drink."

"Like hell you will. Dammit! Get in here!"

By the following morning, Flint was much better. Still a little mellowed out from the medication, he got out of bed, pulled on sweats and sat on the deck for a while, sipping coffee and surveying his land. He had loved this place from the first minute he laid eyes on it. Julie seemed to like it, too. The kids, of course, were crazy about it. He had concluded early on that pleasing the twins went a long way toward making Julie happy. He'd never given much thought to being a father, but he was willing to give it a shot if it meant getting Julie back.

The spread, with its twenty-five acres of solitude, was a great location for writing, and he could be in Los Angeles in less than three hours if necessary. For convenience, he kept an apartment in L.A., but outside of Texas, he figured that Garner Valley was the best place in the world to live. For the first time in his life he had a home, a real home. It only needed Julie to be perfect. He desperately wanted to share his home with her forever.

He heard the back door open and glanced up. Julie. She wore a blue turtleneck sweater the exact color of her eyes. God, she was beautiful. His heart swelled until he thought it might rupture. "Good morning."

She smiled. "Good morning. You must be feeling better."

"Considerably."

"I brought more coffee. May I join you?"

"Of course. Where are the twins?"

"Helping Alma with breakfast." She refilled his mug from the insulated carafe she carried, then filled her own mug.

Flint propped his feet on a deck chair and wrapped his fingers around the mug to warm them. "It's a bit chilly this morning."

"Yes, it is."

"You like it here?"

"Very much."

"How would you—"

"Flint, I need—" They both spoke at the same time.

"Ladies first," he said, smiling.

"Flint, this is very awkward, but I don't know any other way to say it. You have to leave. And this time I mean it."

His smile died. "I thought that we'd been getting along fine."

"Maybe too fine. When you passed out the other day, I was frantic, and the twins were almost hysterical. Later I realized just how much you've insinuated yourself into the children's and my life in a very short time. I don't want that. And I can't say it any plainer than, Leave. Please leave. The sooner, the better."

"But, Julie—"

She held up her hand to shush him. "Now if your back is still bothering you, you can stay until tomorrow morning, or I can make arrangements for a hotel room in town. I'm going to take the children and drive into Palm Springs for an outing. We won't be home until late. It would be easier on the twins if you were gone when we returned."

He stared at her a full thirty seconds before he said, "No. Not just no, but *hell* no. What's with you, Julie? You sound like the heroine of a sappy melodrama. I've told you that I'm not going anywhere until you come to your senses. I love you, and you love me, and if you say any different, you're a liar. Why don't you give us a chance instead of throwing up roadblocks at every opportunity? What are you afraid of?"

"You!" she shouted.

"But why?" he asked, genuinely puzzled. "Honey, trust me. I would never do anything to hurt you."

"Now who's the liar? Flint Durham, I wouldn't trust you as far as I could spit!"

"And you're willing to throw away our shot at happiness without giving us a chance to build something special and lasting?"

"Why not? You did."

"Is that still stuck in your craw? I explained what happened. Honey, I didn't desert you. Believe me, I didn't. I just wanted to make something of myself so I could take care of you. Now I can."

"How? Exactly what do you do to earn a living? I don't want my children living around a dope dealer."

"A dope dealer?" He threw back his head and laughed. "How did you come up with that?"

"Who else carries around a suitcase full of cash?"

"A romantic fool. Honey, I don't deal dope. I told you that I'm a writer, a very successful one."

She eyed him suspiciously. "If you're so successful, then why haven't I heard about your writing?"

He shrugged. "I guess you don't travel in the right circles."

"Show me something that you wrote."

"Tonight, after the kids are in bed, I will."

"Don't play games with me, Flint Durham. By tonight, you'll be gone."

Frustrated, Flint raked his fingers through his hair. "I don't know what more to say, what more to do. Do you want me to get on my knees and beg? Okay, I'll beg." He knelt at her feet and held out his arms in surrender.

She glanced furtively over her shoulder. "Don't be such an idiot, Flint. Someone is going to see you. Get up from there."

"I don't care if the whole world sees me. Julie, give us a chance. Give me some time to prove that you're wrong about me. I swear that you can trust me. I'll never leave you again. Never. I'll swear it on a stack of Bibles a mile high. Look at me, sweetheart." He lifted her chin and gazed deeply into her eyes. "I love you with all my heart and soul. Please give me another chance to prove it. Two weeks. Just give me two weeks. Two weeks without throwing up all your defenses."

He could see the indecision behind her eyes. "Julie, darlin', please. This is my heart we're talking about here." Not above using a little playacting if it would help his case, he clutched his heart and tried to look as pitiful as possible. He stared deeply into her eyes, as if by force of will he could influence her answer.

The back door opened and the boards under his knees shook from two small pairs of running feet.

"Breakfast is ready," Jason called as the twins neared.

Megan cocked her head. "Why are you on your knees? Did you drop something?"

"No, sweetheart," Flint said. "I'm begging your mother to let me stay here."

"Oh, please, Mommy, let him stay. Please, please, please."

"Yeah, Mom, he won't be no trouble," Jason said.

"Any trouble," Julie corrected. To Flint she said, "That's dirty pool."

He shrugged and tried to look innocent.

He watched her waver. It seemed like an eternity before she whispered, "One week. That's all."

A big grin spread across his face. He grabbed her and kissed her hard and quick. "You won't regret this, babe."

She sighed. "Why don't I believe that? And please don't call me babe."

Armed with a detailed map of the area and her destinations clearly marked, Julie hustled Jason and Megan into the back seat of the Jeep and set off for Palm Springs.

As she drove the winding road, she overheard a whispered conversation behind her. "Flint was on his *knees,*" Megan said. "And he kissed Mommy!"

"Yeah. On the mouth. Yuck!"

"Do you know what that means, Jason?"

"Germs?"

"No, silly. It means they're gonna get married."

"And go on a honeymoon? Oh, boy!"

"Don't count on it, kids," Julie said over her shoulder. "Flint and I have no plans to get married."

"Oh, shoot," Jason grumbled. "I wanted a dog."

At the department store that Alma suggested, Julie bought everybody new boots and swimsuits, along with a couple of extra sweaters and sweatshirts for

each of the twins to wear on chilly mornings and eve-
nings.

At lunchtime, they dined at McDonald's.

Julie located a toy store and let the twins pick out
two new board games. Afterward, they bought gifts
for Alma and Javier—and for Flint when the children
insisted—then went to the library for a big supply of
books. At the library, Jason found a flyer for an odd
little museum in Desert Hot Springs and set up a fuss
to go. Julie suspected that it was the mention of a huge
stuffed bear that piqued his interest. The librarian assured them that the place wasn't too far away and that
the children would enjoy visiting the unconventional
home and collection of Cabot Yerxa.

Following the librarian's written directions, she
found the place easily enough. The twins thought that
the odd pueblo and its contents were neat; Julie wasn't
nearly as impressed with the museum or the mangy
stuffed bear as they were. Reminding them that it was
getting late, she coaxed the children away from the
cement and adobe maze with promises of ice cream.

They found a yogurt shop nearby and stopped for
the promised treat. When they got back in the Jeep,
Julie couldn't locate the map. Never mind, she
thought, she remembered the way.

After about fifteen minutes of driving, Megan said,
"Mommy, I think this is the wrong road."

"Oh, no, Megan. I'm sure this is the right one."

"Looks right to me," Jason added.

Megan heaved a dramatic sigh. "We're lost again."

Nine

——

After another fifteen minutes of driving, Julie had to admit that she hadn't seen anything familiar. Worse, the landscape was growing more desolate and the shadows longer. She kept looking for a service station or someplace where she could ask directions.

Nothing.

Finally, she pulled over and stopped. She had passed a few cars on the road, but with all the things going on these days, for safety's sake she didn't dare try to flag down a stranger. "Uh, kids, I think we took a wrong turn."

"Told you," Megan said smugly.

"I'm going to go back the way we came. We'll stop at the first place that looks reputable and get directions."

As she made a U-turn, Jason said, "I'm hungry."

"Love, you just had a chocolate sundae a few minutes ago."

"But my stomach has used it all up."

"We'll get a snack later."

"Promise?"

"Promise."

"I'm sleepy," Megan said.

"Take a nap, pumpkin."

"If I do, you'll get lost again."

"No, I won't."

"Sure?" Megan yawned.

"Pretty sure."

Julie figured that when they left the yogurt shop she had turned right instead of left. All she had to do was go back were she started. She watched the time on the clock and scrupulously retraced her route, expecting to arrive back at the yogurt shop in half an hour.

No yogurt shop.

No Desert Hot Springs.

A sign said, Banning 5 Miles.

Banning?

Oops. Wrong way.

She stopped and turned around again.

Megan roused. "Are we lost again?"

"No, sweetheart. Go back to sleep."

"Maybe I'd better come up front and navigate. It's getting dark. Grandpa says I'm a fine navigator."

"I'm doing okay," she told her daughter. The truth was that she wasn't doing okay at all. She was extremely frustrated. And nervous. She was in a strange part of the country with two small children, it was getting very dark and she was lost as a goose. She was going to have to stop and call somebody.

But who? The telephone number for the house was in her other purse, and she hadn't a clue as to how the phone was listed. Oh, well, she would call the state troopers or whatever they were in California.

She spied a service station on the opposite side of the road and braked quickly. The coast clear, she whipped into the bay.

It was closed.

"Dammit!" She whacked the steering wheel.

"Mom-my," Megan scolded. "You said a bad word."

Sucking in a deep breath, she said evenly, "Yes, I did, dear, and I may say another one very shortly."

Megan giggled.

"Are we home?" Jason said groggily.

"No," Megan told him. "We're lost."

"Not *again*. I'm hungry."

"You're always hungry," Megan said.

"Cause I'm a 'growing boy,' Rosie says."

"Cool it, kids. There's a pay phone by the door. I'm going to call somebody for help."

Jason hung his chin over the front seat. "Flint? I'll bet he would come get us."

"I don't know the phone number there, but I'll call somebody." Julie turned on the overhead light and scratched through her coin purse. She found a quarter, a nickel, three pennies, the back of an earring and a lemon-flavored cough drop. "You kids stay here while I use the phone."

As she started to open the door, Megan said, "I have to use the bathroom."

"Me, too," Jason said.

Julie sighed. "Come on. I'll see if they're open."

They weren't. When Julie suggested that they use nature's facilities, Jason was game, but Megan was horrified at the notion.

"But, Mommy, it's not *private.*"

"Don't be so prissy, Megan. Sometimes we have to improvise."

Reluctantly, Megan concurred.

That business concluded, Julie took the quarter and went to the pay phone. She lifted the receiver, deposited the coin and punched zero.

Nothing happened.

She punched it again. And again. Still nothing. She slammed the receiver back on the hook and waited for her quarter. It didn't appear. She jiggled the hook. No quarter. The darned thing was as dead as a doornail.

So much for a phone call.

"I'm hungry," Jason said. "Can I have one of these?" He pointed to a vending machine filled with candy bars and other goodies.

"I'm thirsty," Megan said, eyeing the soft drink machine. "I want a Coke."

"Sorry kids, no coins. Come on. At least we know the way to Banning. Wherever that is."

Julie hated getting lost, but she had an absolutely lousy sense of direction. That's why she always carried a good map along with her. She was great at reading maps.

Good Lord. There was probably a map in the car.

There was. In the door pocket. Plain as day.

Well, no wonder she was so lost. She'd gone north and east instead of south and west. Feeling much better about the situation, she started the Jeep and pulled out of the bay. The vehicle lurched and jumped in a peculiar way until she stopped and got out. It was too dark to see the extent of the damage.

"Megan, look in the glove compartment and see if there is a flashlight."

There was. And her right rear tire was flat as a flitter. She didn't have a clue as to how to change it.

"Kids, it looks like we're stuck here for the night."

"I'm hungry."

"I'm thirsty."

Julie rummaged around for a nice-sized rock.

Megan licked chocolate from her fingers. "Let's sing 'Six Little Ducks' again."

"Honey, please, why don't you just go to sleep?"

"I'm not sleepy at all. This is fun. Like camping out."

"Yeah," Jason said. "Let's tell ghost stories."

"I don't think so," Julie said. "Are you two warm enough?" Besides being wrapped in a plaid blanket they found in the back, both the kids had on an extra sweatshirt and sweater from their new clothes, and Julie was wearing the sweatshirt that the twins had picked out for Flint. It had a bear on the front.

She had tried to keep up a brave front for the twins, but it was after midnight, and she was very aware of their vulnerability. "I'd give anything for a phone right now."

"There's one in the glove compartment," Megan said.

"One what?"

"Telephone. A cell'ar one like you have at home."

"Why didn't you tell me?" Julie shrieked.

"I don't know," Megan said in a very small voice trembling with tears.

"I'm sorry, honey. I'm sorry I yelled. Mommy is upset, but not at you." Julie quickly retrieved the phone. It was almost exactly like hers. She had special numbers programmed on hers. She prayed this one did, too, as she punched the recall button.

Flint was frantic. His first thought was that Julie had run away again. His second was that she and the kids had been hurt. He'd called every hospital and every law enforcement agency in the area. He had drunk a dozen cups of coffee and had paced the floor for hours. He'd snapped at Alma and Javier, who hadn't done a damned thing.

Alma, her eyes swollen, prayed in Spanish and twisted her apron into a wrinkled wad. Flint knew that both she and Javier were also worried about Julie and the twins.

When the phone rang, Flint grabbed it. "Hello!"

"Uh, who is this?" a voice asked hesitantly.

"Julie, it's Flint. Are you all right? Where are you?"

As she filled him in on the situation, he could tell that she was scared and embarrassed. "I'll be there as quick as I can, babe. By helicopter if I can manage it. Just sit tight."

Flint rousted Kyle out of bed and bullied him into flying out to where Julie was stranded.

"You owe me one for this, buddy," Kyle said, "and you'd better be damned glad there's a full moon."

Time seemed to drag by until they spotted the Jeep. Julie must have heard them since the headlights started flashing on and off. As soon as the chopper set down, Flint jumped out and dashed toward the Cherokee. She was out of the vehicle and waiting for him.

He grabbed her and kissed her face a dozen times. "Don't ever do that to me again. I've been frantic. I was scared to death that you'd run away from me again and out of my mind when I thought that you might be hurt." He crushed her to him in a bear hug.

"Flint, I can't breathe."

"Sorry." He loosened his hold but slid an arm around her waist and hugged her to his side. After the fright he'd had, he wanted to keep her close to him. He felt a tug on his pant leg and looked down.

Jason, his mouth smeared with something dark, grinned up at him and said, "We've been having a 'venture."

"Yeah," Megan said. "Mommy got lost, but she said not to worry. Even when we got hungry and thirsty and didn't have any more quarters."

"She picked up a big rock and went *ka-blooie!*" Jason smacked his fist in his opposite palm for effect. "And we had crackers and candy bars and juice. Boy, it was neat!"

Flint glanced over at the front of the station and couldn't help laughing. "*You* wasted the vending machines?"

"I did."

"It was a 'mergency," Jason explained.

"But we're prepared to make rest—rest—" Megan looked up at her mother.

"Restitution."

"Restitution. That means we have to pay for what we broke and what we ate. Mommy put a note under the door."

"How about we get out of here?" Flint asked. "We'll fly back with Dr. Kyle."

"Wow!" Jason said. "In a helicopter? Wow!"

"What about the Jeep?" Julie asked.

"We'll lock it, and I'll have somebody fix it tomorrow. Let's go home."

When Julie looked at the clock the next morning, she couldn't believe the time. She hadn't slept until ten for ages—certainly not since the twins were born. She showered, dressed quickly and went downstairs.

Flint and the twins were sitting in the middle of the floor with all sorts of fishing gear. Flint was wearing the bear sweatshirt that the kids had selected for him.

Megan spotted Julie first. "Hi, Mommy. We're going fishing."

"Yeah," Jason said. "We're going to practice in the swimming pool first, and this afternoon we're going to fish in a boat in a lake."

"Want to come along?" Flint asked innocently.

The dog. He knew perfectly well that she'd always hated boats and water. "I'll pass. And I don't think that it's a good idea for the children to go, either."

The kids set up a howl of protests. "Why not?"

"Hush, kids," Flint said. "I should have asked your mother's permission first. She isn't very fond of water."

"She isn't?" Megan asked, as if it surprised her.

"I apologize, Julie. But you should know that I'll take very good care of them. They're good swimmers, and they'll be in life jackets the whole time."

"Please, Mommy. Please, please, please, please."

"I'll think about it."

Jason opened his mouth to protest, but Flint touched his shoulder and shook his head. The protest died. Julie wished that she could quash her son's mulishness so easily.

"Mommy," Megan said, "Flint loves his shirt. I tiptoed into your room and got it. It has chocolate on it, but he says he doesn't mind."

"It smells like you." Flint raised his arm to sniff the sleeve, then looked up, his dark eyes smoldering with hidden meaning.

Julie knew that look. And she remembered the countless times he had nuzzled her neck and kissed it, whispered in her ear, "God, I love the way you smell. It sets me on fire."

Unbidden, her hand went to her neck and rubbed it. As soon as she realized what she'd done, she snatched it away. When she heard a soft chuckle, she glanced at Flint. He smiled and winked.

Damn him!

"I—I'm going to get a cup of coffee."

Flint nodded. "Is it okay if we practice fishing in the pool?"

"It's fine." She hurried from the room.

When the children came running inside later that day, their faces beaming, Julie was glad that she'd relented and let them go fishing with Flint. After all, the man had been a professional fishing guide.

"Mommy, Mommy, come look."

"We caught lots and lots of fish. Come see."

With a twin tugging on each hand, she went outside. They dropped her hands, ran to an insulated
chest and lifted out a big stringer of fish. Their small
legs almost buckled under the weight. Flint grinned
and lent a hand.

"I'm impressed," Julie said.

"Flint said we were naturals," Jason said, his thin
chest puffing up.

"Yeah, and we're going to eat them for dinner. But
first we have to clean them and take out all their insides," Megan said, wrinkling her nose.

"Don't be such a sissy," Jason told his sister. "If we
catch them, we clean them. That's what Flint said."

Julie glanced anxiously at Flint. "I don't think they
should be handling sharp knives."

"Don't worry about it. I'll be the only one with a
knife."

"Yep," Jason said. "We're the assistants. I'm in
charge of the bag of the parts we don't eat."

"And I'm in charge of the bowl of parts that we do
eat." Megan looked proud enough of herself to pop.

A few hours later, the fish had been cleaned, cooked
and eaten. Everyone had declared them the best fish
they had ever tasted, and Flint, Julie, and the twins
settled down to play the newest board game Jason had
selected.

As the children's bedtime approached, Julie began
to grow more and more nervous. She didn't ordinarily go to bed at nine o'clock, but, truthfully, she was
nervous about being left alone with Flint. She glanced

at him, and her anxiety level almost went off the chart. He was giving her another one of those looks—the kind that magnetized her eyes to his and said, "I want to run my tongue over every inch of your body and make love to you until you cry for mercy."

Or maybe she was projecting her own thoughts into the interpretation. Heat flushed up her throat, crept past her chin and spread over her face. Her cheeks felt blistered; a sheen of perspiration formed on her forehead. The children and the game they played faded into the background. Like a pair of charmed cobras, blue eyes and black eyes were locked in a world of sensual memories, swaying to an enchanted flute.

"Hot?" he asked softly.

"Sweltering," she whispered.

"Let's walk out on the deck and cool off."

She started to rise.

"Mommy, Mommy," Megan said, impatiently tugging at Julie's slacks. "You can't leave. The game's not over. It's your move."

She blinked and stared at Megan. So caught up in Flint's magic was she, that it took her a moment to return to earth. "My move?"

Megan sighed impatiently. "You have the dice in your hand."

Julie uncurled her fingers and looked down at her palm. Snake eyes stared back at her. She flung the dice onto the board as if they burned her hand and refused to look at Flint again.

When it was time for the children to go upstairs, she meant to go with them, but when she tried to beat a quick exit, Flint caught her wrist.

"Why such a hurry?" he asked. He gave her a slow, sexy smile that reeked of damp bodies and tangled sheets. "I have something I want to show you."

"I'll bet you do." She tried to twist from his grasp, but he held her firmly. "Well, you can just keep it in your pants."

He let out a bark of laughter. "That wasn't what I had in mind. I promised to show you some of my writing."

"Oh." A different kind of heat flushed her face. "May I have a rain check on that? I'm sort of tired tonight."

He looked amused, but his bedroom eyes challenged her. "Chick-en," he taunted softly.

Her spine stiffened. "Very well. As soon as the children are tucked in, I'll be back down."

"I'll light the fire and pour us a brandy."

"Flint, I agreed to read your work, not share a romantic evening."

"It's not exactly the kind of— Never mind. I'll explain when you come back."

Ten

Julie pressed a cool washcloth to her face, trying to lower her temperature and get her emotions under control. Promising to let Flint stay for a week was a huge mistake. Unadulterated idiocy. A lack of passion between them had never been a problem. They struck sparks off each other by merely breathing the same air. The years apart seemed only to have heightened the phenomenon.

No, the chemistry was there, definitely there. Always had been. It was all the other stuff that was the problem. It was a crying shame that she couldn't have combined the best parts of Rob and Flint.

Rob was conscientious, dependable and steady as a rock. But there hadn't been that special element, that... chemistry. She'd tried to convince herself that a marriage between them would work, but she knew now that it wouldn't have. Uncle William had recognized it and tried to talk her out of marrying Rob, but she and her parents had been so sure that Rob was perfect. Rob had never made her toes curl or her heart sing.

Not like Flint.

But if Flint took a wild notion to leave, she had no doubt that he'd be off without a backward glance. All his protests to the contrary, if he'd done it before, he would do it again. Could she live like that? More important, could she ask her children to live like that?

She wanted the twins to have a stable home in a good neighborhood and a healthy environment where they could grow up safe and happy. An apartment in L.A. didn't sound anywhere close to what she had in mind.

On the other hand—

Leaning on the bathroom sink, Julie stared at her image in the mirror. "Honey, you've landed yourself in one mell of a hess."

She applied a quick coat of lip gloss, ran her fingers through her hair and went downstairs to face the inevitable.

Logs crackled in the fireplace. The lights were low. Two brandy snifters waited on the coffee table. Flint held out his hand to her. "Come sit by me on the couch."

She chose a distant wing chair. "I'll be more comfortable here."

"But you can't see the TV from there."

"We're going to watch TV? I thought I was going to look at your writing."

"We are. Come over here, and I'll explain." He patted the couch beside him.

Reluctantly, she rose and joined him on the couch, but she sat much farther away than the place he had patted. He merely looked amused and handed her a snifter of brandy.

"Thank you." She took a polite sip. "What's on TV?"

"A movie. It's in the VCR. It's called *Bad Blues Heat.* Came out almost four years ago. Ever seen it?"

She shook her head. "But the title seems familiar. What's it about?"

"It's an action-adventure set in New Orleans featuring a couple of tough homicide cops."

"Oh, I remember reading about it, but it's not the kind of movie I usually go to see. It's sort of a Southern style *Lethal Weapon,* isn't it?"

He chuckled. "Bite your tongue. But that's the one. It wasn't nominated for an Oscar, but it was a big box-office success. The sequel came out last year. Mind watching a little of this one with me?"

She shrugged. "I suppose not, but if it gets too gory, may I close my eyes?"

"Sure. I'll warn you ahead of time." He punched the remote control and the TV came to life.

Turning to him, she said, "Flint, if you've already seen this, I'd really rather watch something less vio—"

"Shh. Watch the credits."

She concentrated on the screen for a few moments, watching a scene on a misty, dark street with the sound of Dixieland music in the background. A laughing red-haired woman reeled out of a bar and staggered down the dark street alone. Suddenly a gloved left hand covered her mouth. The woman's eyes widened as she struggled and made muffled noises. A gloved right hand holding a sinister-looking knife started a slashing motion.

Julie clamped her eyes shut and ducked her head as some character screamed bloody murder. The whine of police sirens overlaid the jazz sounds. Julie drew her feet up and rested her forehead on her knees.

"Oh, shoot, you missed it," Flint said.

Using her hand to shield the movie from her line of vision Julie glanced toward him. "I really don't want to watch this if you don't mind. It's too bloody for me. I thought we were going to look at your work tonight."

"We are. This is it."

She frowned. "What are you talking about?"

"Here, let me rewind the tape, and I'll show you." He fiddled with the remote control for a moment, then said, "The scary part is over. Watch."

She squinted at the screen, concentrating on police cars speeding through streets, sirens screaming and a crowd gathering as the title and opening credits rolled. "What am I watching for?"

"There!"

"Where? What?"

"You missed it." He manipulated the remote's buttons again, backing up the tape slowly, then pausing the frame. "There. Read it."

"Screenplay by John Anthony Durham." Puzzled, she studied the screen. It took a couple of beats for the information to soak in. She turned to Flint. "That's *you.*"

He was grinning from ear to ear. "Yep."

"You wrote the screenplay for *Bad Blues Heat?*"

"I sure did. Three of Hollywood's macho stars wanted it, and I made a pile of money on the deal."

"Holy Hannah!" She could only stare at him, stunned. "Is that where you got the money in the suitcase?"

"Nope. I got that for the treatment of *Bad Blues Heat III.*"

"What's a treatment?"

"Sort of a summary of the planned screenplay."

She was still stunned. Flint, her Flint, aka John Anthony Durham, wrote movies. "You really are a writer."

"I really am."

"Well, tell me about it. How did it happen?"

Flint stretched out with his feet on the coffee table and his brandy snifter resting on his belly. "The fall before I left, I entered a contest that was part of a writer's conference in Beaumont. I won in my category. The other screenplay finalists must have been abysmal because from the way the judge tore mine up, I had a lot to learn. The judge of the screenplay division was a teacher at UCLA, and he said that he thought I had a lot of potential and encouraged me to apply for a scholarship to study at the film school. With all the competition, I didn't figure that I stood a chance, but I wanted that scholarship so badly that I could taste it.''

"And you got it," Julie said quietly.

"And I got it. The letter came the day before we were supposed to get married. I don't think you could ever understand how desperately I wanted to be able to make something of myself, to be able to support you in style. When that letter came, it looked like the answer to my prayers—a year of free study with the greatest filmmakers in the world. I couldn't believe it. I was dumbstruck.''

"Why didn't you just tell me about it?"

"Now, looking back, I don't know. It seems stupid that I didn't, but at the time I was too insecure about my writing. You can't believe how competitive the field is. What if I failed? I longed to be someone you could be proud of. Too, I wasn't completely sure that the whole thing wasn't some sort of mistake or a dream that I would wake up from. I decided that I would go to California and check it out, then tell you. And I did write you about it. I wrote and called many times.''

Julie sighed. "But I didn't get the letters. Or the phone calls."

"And the next thing I knew, you were married."

Tears welled up in her eyes and spilled over. "Oh, Flint. If you'd only told me the truth. I thought that you didn't love me."

"Shh, darlin'." He gathered her into his arms and rubbed his cheek against hers, drying the tears. "I loved you. I've always loved you." Gently he kissed the corners of her eyes.

Then he kissed her nose.

And her chin.

When his mouth covered hers, she thought she would melt and run between the sofa cushions. His lips were unbelievably soft and sensuous. His large hand moved up the length of her leg, over her hip, paused at her waist, then continued a maddeningly slow journey to the side of her breast. He rubbed the swell with the heel of his hand, then slid it underneath and cupped her with his splayed fingers.

She sighed against his lips, and they nudged hers wider as his tongue thrust hotly. She buried her fingers in his long, thick hair, pulled his mouth even closer and returned the wild thrusting.

He groaned.

She moaned.

Small fingers tapped urgently on her shoulder. "Mom. Mom."

Julie tore her mouth from Flint's and blinked at her son, who looked thoroughly disgusted.

"You were *kissing* again," Jason said, his nose wrinkling. "On the *mouth*."

"I'll say this for him," Flint said, "the kid's got good eyesight."

Embarrassed, Julie quickly sat up and fluffed her hair. "Jason, why are you out of bed?"

"I'm not sleepy. I heard a police siren down here. Are ya'll watching a movie? I want to watch, too." He wedged himself between Julie and Flint and wiggled and squirmed until he was comfortably situated. Then he picked up the remote control and punched a button. The screen image jumped from a silent still frame to raucous action with police cars screaming and ambulances blaring. "Wow," Jason said, his eyes enormous. "Wow. Look at all the blood. Wow. This is great."

Julie shook her head. "I can't believe that this ghoulish creature is my child."

Flint laughed and leaned back with his fingers laced behind his head. "The kid's got fantastic taste."

Despite Jason's assertion that he wasn't sleepy, in five minutes, his eyes began to droop. He snuggled against his mother, sighed and went sound asleep.

With the backs of his fingers Flint brushed the breast where Jason's head lay. "Boy," he said, winking at Julie, "some guys have all the luck."

Julie stepped into her high heels and checked her outfit in the mirror. Flint had told her to put on something fancy for dinner, and she had. The red silk slip dress and embroidered jacket were part of her trousseau. Her hands ran down the curves of her hips, savoring the feel of the sensuous material. Closing her eyes, she could almost feel Flint's hands trace the same path.

Yes. She admitted it. She wanted him. Soon. His week had stretched into ten days, and he'd spent almost every waking minute entertaining her and the twins. They had gone riding. They had gone picnicking. They had gone exploring in museums, deserts and mountains. They had gone to movies, ice rinks and ice cream parlors.

But they hadn't gone to bed. Not just the two of them. Not to make love.

Oh, there had been a few steamy kisses. Well . . . more than a few. But Flint always stopped short. She assumed it was part of a game he was playing—keeping her hot and bothered until he wore down her defenses.

A secret smile played at the corners of her lips as she touched a dab of perfume between her breasts. Well, two could play that game. Her defenses were long gone, and by the time they came home tonight, Flint Durham would be ripping off his clothes before he hit the door.

Tonight's the night.

She put on her diamond earrings and took a last look in the mirror. A sudden notion worried her. Was she overdressed? Flint had never been one to dress up. He preferred cowboy boots and Levi's. They used to joke that, to him, going formal meant putting a crease in his jeans and polishing his belt buckle.

Nibbling at her lip, she considered changing.

No, there wasn't time.

The moment she went down and saw Flint waiting at the foot of the stairs, she was glad she hadn't changed. This was a Flint she'd never seen before. When he smiled up at her, he almost took her breath away.

He wore a black suit in a European cut that boasted of custom-tailoring. His shirt was silk, as was his subdued tie. His shoes looked Italian. His dark hair was slicked back and caught at his nape with a small silver clasp. He exuded confidence and style, and sexuality pulsated from him like the roar of an outbound jet.

Her knees went weak just from looking at him. And when his gaze caressed her slowly from her toes to her upswept hair, her skin came alive with sensation, and she held on to the banister to keep from stumbling.

When she stood before him, he raised her hand to his lips. "Exquisite. I will be the envy of every man at the restaurant."

"Thank you." She smiled. "And I suspect all the ladies would gladly change places with me. You look very handsome."

He winked. "Over the past few years I've learned to clean up pretty good. Shall we go?"

"Let me say goodbye to the kids."

The twins were engrossed in a puzzle, but when they saw Flint and Julie, they both grinned and glanced at each other as if in conspiracy.

"What are you two hatching?" Julie asked.

"You look beautiful, Mommy," Megan said, side-stepping the question.

"Yeah, beau-ti-ful," added Jason. "Are you and Flint going on a *date?*"

"Well, we're going to dinner. I want you both to be on your best behavior for Alma. Okay?"

"Okay."

"'Kay. Mom, are you and Flint going on a honeymoon pretty soon?"

Megan elbowed her brother. "I told you not to say that. It's very rude."

Saved by her daughter, Julie thought. After good-night hugs all around, Flint escorted her out the front door. Outside sat a sleek black Jaguar. Julie's brows went up.

"Whose car is this?" she asked as Flint helped her in.

"I borrowed it from Kyle Rutledge."

Her hand slid over the soft leather seat. "*Very* nice."

"If you like it, I'll buy you one."

"Flint, I wasn't hinting, I was merely admiring something beautiful. This isn't a practical car for a mother with two five-year-olds."

"True. Maybe when they're older."

Julie started to chastise him again, then let it pass. Several times in the past few days, he'd surprised her with things that she'd casually admired on their outings with the kids—a silver bracelet, a desert painting by a local artist. He'd even come in one day wagging a bedspread that had caught her eye in a shop window. She'd learned to keep her complimentary comments to herself.

She certainly didn't want a Jaguar, but she didn't want to begin the evening by criticizing his behavior, either. As they drove, she turned the conversation to more neutral topics such as catching him up on the news about mutual acquaintances in Travis Creek. Soon they were laughing together about the antics of some of the town's more colorful characters.

By the time they reached Palm Springs, night had fallen and the town was ablaze with light. Flint pulled the Jag under the awning of what appeared to be an extremely classy restaurant.

"We're going to eat *here?*"

"If I promise not to eat my peas with a fish knife, will it be acceptable?"

Julie felt herself blush. "I didn't mean . . . that."

Chuckling, he leaned over and kissed her. "I know, sweetheart. I was only teasing."

Her door opened and a uniformed attendant helped her out. When the young man spotted Flint, a smile split his freckled face. "Hey, there, Mr. D. I didn't recognize you with these wheels."

"The Jag belongs to Dr. Rutledge, Pete. So don't put any dings—"

Pete laughed and held up his hands. "Gotcha. I know Dr. Rutledge."

Flint escorted her to the door, opened it and touched her back lightly as he guided her inside the restaurant. For a moment, Julie was sure that they had entered a movie set. The room was magnificent. Opulent. Slightly understated opulence, but opulent nonetheless—as only Louis XIV styles can be.

When the very proper-looking maître d' glimpsed them, he actually clicked his heels before he bowed. Julie bit the inside of her lip to keep from giggling. She could only imagine Flint's reaction to the fellow.

"Ah, Mr. Durham, we're delighted to have you dine with us this evening. I have reserved an excellent table for you and the mademoiselle."

"Thanks, Bernard."

"This way please."

As the maître d' turned to lead them, Julie shot Flint an eyebrows-raised look that clearly said, "I'm surprised that you and Bernard are so obviously well acquainted."

The shrug he returned said just as clearly, "Ain't no big thing, babe."

As they traversed the room, Flint exchanged nods with several people, people who seemed vaguely familiar. As they approached one table, a dark-haired man stood, gave a lopsided smile and stuck out his hand. "John, my man, it's been a while. How's it going? And who's this beautiful new lady?"

Flint muttered a greeting and shook hands with the man, then turned to her and slid his arm possessively around her waist, and calmly introduced her to one of the biggest box office hunks in Hollywood. Smiling down at her, Flint said, "This is Julie Stevens, the great love of my life."

Stunned speechless to see the star in person, Julie managed some semblance of a smile.

"Ho." The film tough guy laughed and clapped Flint on the back. "Then I guess you're not interested in joining our table?"

"Thanks, another time." Flint nodded to the others at the table, and parted with a two-finger wave.

Bernard had paused and was waiting patiently. As they continued to their table, Julie was still stunned. "That was—that was—"

"Yep."

Bernard stopped at a table set with dazzling white linens, gleaming crystal and a footed vase of cascading pink lilies. He held the damask-and-gilt chair for Julie to be seated, offered menus from a waiter who suddenly materialized and murmured to Flint that the wine steward would be along shortly.

"I thought he would be taller," Julie said quietly.

"Who?"

"'Who?' he says. I'm talking about the movie star you just introduced me to. I can't believe that you know him. He seems very nice.''

Flint shrugged. "Honey, because of my work I've met a lot of celebrities in the past few years. Believe me, movie stars are just ordinary folks like you and me. Some are nice and some are jerks.''

Julie leaned closer. "Are there any other celebrities here?''

He glanced around. "A few." A blonde at a nearby table caught his eye. She scrunched up her shoulders, smiled broadly and wiggled her fingers. Flint returned her greeting.

Julie did a double take when she recognized the star of a popular T.V. sitcom. "Do you know her, too?'' When he nodded, she said, "I'm still surprised that you seem to know so many people here. It seems strange.''

"Not so strange. As I said, I meet lots of celebrities because of my work—which doesn't make me big dog, believe me. In Hollywood, screenwriters are low in the pecking order.''

"No, I didn't mean just the celebrities. You seem to know the valet and the maître d', and they obviously know you. You must come here often.''

Before Flint could respond, the wine steward and a waiter approached with an iced bottle of wine. While the waiter set up the silver bucket, the steward placed crystal flutes on the table.

Flint frowned. "But I didn't order—"

The steward handed him a note. "From the gentleman across the room, sir." He offered the bottle for the label to be observed. "Dom Perignon. And an excellent year."

Flint read the note, passed it to Julie, then glanced at the star, who gave one of his famous grins along with a thumbs-up. Flint answered in kind.

Congratulations, the note had said. *You're a lucky man.*

The champagne was like liquid sunshine, and its effervescence set the mood for the rest of the evening. The food was delicious, Flint was attentive and entertaining and the electricity between them was unbelievable.

An intimate awareness heated the air and seemed to cocoon them in a translucent sphere of libidinous energy so sensual and so potent that it rivaled a nuclear reactor.

As the *crème brûlé* was being served, Julie, feeling totally decadent, slipped off her jacket. Flint's blatant leer went immediately to the bodice of her slip dress. She stretched slightly, knowing full well the impact her breasts moving against the silk would have on him.

She was right. He almost choked on his coffee.

"Are you wearing anything under that dress?"

She traced a figure eight on the back of his hand and smiled provocatively. "Not a stitch."

His cup clattered against the saucer. "Let's get out of here." He stood and held out his hand.

"But what about dessert?" she asked, feigning wide-eyed innocence.

"We'll get a doggie bag."

Eleven

———

The powerful car roared up the mountain highway with Flint clutching the wheel tightly, his total concentration on the twists and turns of the road. Driving like a man possessed—or rather obsessed—he hadn't said a word in the half hour or so since they'd left the restaurant. In the dim glow of the dash instruments, Julie could see that his jaw was tightly clamped.

"You look absolutely grim," she told him. "What's wrong?"

He braked, whipped into one of the wide vista points off the highway and stopped. "I was trying to make it home, but I don't think I can. I want you so damned bad that the top of my head is about to blow off. Come here. At least let me kiss you."

He quickly threw off his seat belt and fumbled with hers. "Here," she said, laughing, "let me."

When she was freed, he gathered her into his arms and kissed her with a fervid urgency that had her gasping. His tongue took what the rest of him could not yet have. Hooking his thumbs in the straps of her dress, he peeled down jacket and bodice until her breasts were bare. With a groan, he moved his face over her breasts, brushing, kissing, flicking her nipples with his tongue. "I thought I was going to go crazy wanting to do this."

"I thought I was going to go crazy with wanting you to do it," she whispered.

He tried to move closer, then cursed. "Damned bucket seats. I wish we were in my Cherokee." Breathing raggedly, he nipped his way up her throat to her mouth.

"I thought you had an Explorer," she said as his lips teased hers.

"Whatever." He kissed her again. "Let's get out of here. Jag's weren't designed for making love."

"There's always the back seat." She clasped the back of his head and brought his mouth back to her breasts.

"It's getting too cold without the heater," he murmured against her skin, "and it's too dangerous to run it." His hand slid up the sleek length of her leg from ankle to thigh. "I thought you said you weren't wearing any underwear."

"Only panty hose. And they're very, very sheer."

He shook his head and made a huge bear noise. "Let's get home before I strip you naked and freeze your tootsie off."

Julie tried to protest that her tootsie wouldn't freeze, but he resolutely restored her dress, her jacket and her seat belt.

"Sugar, what I have in mind is gonna take a lot of time and a lot of room." He fired up the Jag and roared off.

Sexual energy filled the car, spitting and sparking like a cut electric cable snaking and bouncing off wet pavement. She wanted to jam her foot on the brake, drag him from his seat and make love with him in the middle of the road. Desire pulsated low in her body, and she squirmed in her seat. "Hurry," she whispered.

"I'm driving as fast as I can without risking our necks. I don't want to crash over the side of the mountain. Not now."

She laughed. "Aren't we a pair?"

He grinned. "A perfect pair."

Finally, they reached the house. Two seat belts clicked apart; two doors opened and closed rapidly; two pairs of feet hit the front steps at the same time. Two hands reached for the doorknob, bumping and fumbling until they got tickled.

Julie acquiesced, letting him do the honors.

"Damn, it's locked. Where's the key?"

"I don't have it. I thought you had it."

"Damn." He poked the doorbell impatiently. Once. Twice. Then three times rapidly.

The door finally opened. Alma, looking a little sleepy, smiled broadly. "Ah, Señor Ju—"

"Thanks, Alma," Flint said quickly, pulling Julie inside. "You can go home now." He struck out for the master bedroom, Julie in tow and having to trot to keep up with his long strides.

"Okay," Alma said, scurrying along beside them. "The *niños* are asleep in their beds upstairs. Like little angels they look."

"Fine, Alma. Thank you." When they reached the door to the master suite, he turned and said sharply. "Thank you, Alma. Good night."

Startled, the housekeeper glanced at Julie, who was trying furiously not to laugh, then back at Flint. "Ahh, *sí*," she said, ducking her head to hide her smile. *"Buenas noches, señor, señora."*

The moment that the door was closed behind them, Flint impatiently ripped off his jacket and tie, tossed them aside and reached for Julie's jacket. She was one step ahead of him. Her silk jacket was already puddled on the floor, and she had stepped out of her shoes.

In the soft glow of a dim bedside lamp, she could see his eyes blaze and his nostrils flare as she reached for the straps of her dress.

"Wait," he said, "let me." He started unbuttoning his shirt.

She smiled and stepped closer. "Let me." She quickly had it off. Her hands stroked circles over his bare shoulders and chest, then reached for his belt. His thumbs tugged at her straps, but she brushed them away. "Wait. First you."

When his last garment was shed, and the finely carved man stood before her, splendidly tumescent, Julie unfastened his hair and tossed the silver clasp aside. He shook his head, and that great dark mane spread over his broad shoulders, transforming him into a magnificent savage. She made a little growling noise in the back of her throat and, catlike, rubbed her body against his.

Flint went wild.

In one fluid motion, the red silk dress was over her head and fluttering to a chair. In another fluid motion, her panty hose were down to her ankles. Crouching before her, he tapped one foot; she lifted it. He tapped the other foot; she lifted it. The wisp of nylon sailed off to meet the dress.

Squatting with his feet planted outside of hers, his hands went to the backs of her legs. Slowly, very slowly, he rose, his tongue leading the way upward, licking a wet trail and pausing in some very provocative places. His hands stroked a path up her calves, her thighs, her bottom, her back, and pressed her against his body as it writhed upward over hers until he was standing.

She almost lost it. Julie had never experienced anything so erotic in her entire life. She must have been carrying on like crazy because Flint chuckled and said, "Like that?"

"What's not to like?" she gasped. And darned if he didn't do it again.

She closed her eyes, grabbed great handfuls of his hair to keep from crumpling into shards of sensation and savored every seductive moment. By the time he reached her mouth again, she would have sold state secrets or confessed to killing Cock Robin in a flash.

Thank heavens he picked her up and carried her to the bed. She couldn't walk. She couldn't have moved if her life depended on it.

Half a minute later, she discovered that was a lie. His fingers slid between her thighs, and she *moved*. She moved like a wild woman.

"Now," she begged between fiery kisses. "I'm dying."

"Me, too," he panted. "Let's die together." He thrust deeply inside her.

She went even wilder, kissing and clawing and thrashing. She was a teeming mass of raw nerve endings alive with primal excitement and glistening with the sheen of carnal need. In a frenzied race to fulfillment that burned inferno hot and slicked their bodies with the sweat of it, they stroked and strove, reaching...reaching...reaching.

Her climax exploded in a fury. With her first spasm, he stiffened, then uttered a guttural cry and bowed his back as his own broke and pumped from him.

For several moments they lay there, still, not speaking.

Her skin cooled.

His weight grew heavy.

"Flint?" she whispered.

Nothing.

She shook him. "Flint? Are you dead?"

"As a mackerel," he mumbled.

"Well, move. You're getting heavy."

"I can't. Just throw some dirt over me and plant a few petunias."

She giggled and tickled his sides. That moved him. In a hurry. He'd always been ticklish. He pinned her arms and rolled to his back, drawing her on top of him. She laid her cheek on his chest and twirled a strand of his damp dark hair around her finger. "That was good, wasn't it?"

"No, sugar, that wasn't good—that was unbelievable. And I'm beginning to wonder if it's a good idea for us to get married."

She lifted her head and looked at him. "You are?"

He grinned. "I don't think my heart could take too many nights like this one."

"Oh, I suppose, then, that I'd better start looking around for someone with a stronger constitution."

"Like hell you will!" He flipped her onto her back and leaned over her. "Sweetheart, if I gotta die, it might as well be while I'm trying to make you happy."

She laughed. "I don't think you want to marry me. You just want my body."

"That, too. But I do want to marry you, love." He kissed the tip of her nose. "I want us to get married and live happily ever after."

"You forget that I have two children."

"They're great kids, Julie. I'm crazy about them. In fact," he said, a wistfulness drifting across his features, "I wish to hell they were mine."

She almost told him then. Almost. But a tiny little niggle of doubt told her to wait. There was time yet.

His lips brushed hers in a quick kiss, then lingered.

A spark caught.

A flame flared.

"Oh, Flint," she moaned.

"Oh, babe," he groaned.

Teased by the light filtering through the blinds, Julie awakened slowly, then drifted in and out, savoring the warmth of the covers pulled up to her nose and of the body pressed against her back. She snuggled against him and enjoyed the delicious languor that comes after a night of lovemaking.

He pressed closer, fanning his large hand over her belly, then sliding it lower to cup the spot made supersensitive after their vigorous encounters.

"I think her eyes moved," a young voice whispered.

"Do you think she's awake?" whispered another.

Julie's eyes flew open. Two familiar faces, chins propped on palms, stared at her. "What are you kids doing in here?" she shrieked, scrambling to make sure that she and Flint were adequately covered.

"Waitin' for you to get through sleeping," Jason said.

"Alma said we was to be very quiet and not wake you up to ask if Flint could take us fishing. Is he awake yet?"

Flint stirred and raised up. "What are you two doing in here?"

"I've already been through that," Julie said. "They want to go fishing."

"Maybe later," he said, his head dropping like a rock to the pillow. "After a shower. After coffee. After a couple more hours of sleep."

"Whatcha doin' sleeping in Flint's bed, Mom?" Jason asked, his elbows still resting on the side of the mattress, his cupped chin only inches from her face. "Did you have a bad dream?"

"Not exactly."

"Mommy, did you know that there's a big painting of you on that wall?" Megan pointed to the wall opposite the bed. "And you're *naked*," she whispered loudly.

"No, honey, it's not me," she mumbled against the pillow, wanting nothing so desperately as some more sleep. "Why don't you guys go watch some cartoons or something?"

"There's only news stuff on TV," Jason said. "And it is, too, you, Mom. And in that picture you don't have on *any* clothes at all. Not even any *socks*."

She felt Flint stiffen beside. "Julie, honey..."

Julie slowly lifted her head. As she stared at the opposite wall, her eyes widened and she almost swallowed her tongue. "Oh...my...God."

There, in living color and bigger than life, was an enormous oil painting of Julie draped over a velvet chaise. And the twins were right. She didn't have a thing on. Not even any socks.

She wanted to cover her children's eyes. She wanted to cover her own eyes.

Anger and embarrassment flared through her. "Kids, out of here! Now."

"But, Mom—"

Clutching the comforter to her bosom, Julie thrust a finger toward the door. "Out. Now. March!"

With much foot-dragging, the twins left the room. As soon as the door closed, Julie sprang from the bed, jerking the bulky comforter off Flint and wrapping it around herself.

Gesticulating furiously toward the painting, Julie shrieked, "Where did that...that *tawdry* abomination come from?"

He started crawling across the bed toward her. "Honey, I can explain—"

She took a step backward. Ablaze with righteous indignation, she stiffened her spine and lifted her chin. "I'd like to hear your *explanation*. I've never posed for such a vulgar display in my entire life."

"A friend of mine painted it from some snapshots and my memory. I think it's damned good myself."

He might as well have poured gasoline on a brush fire as to have said that. Steam came out her ears. "I think it's disgusting. And my *children* saw it. Oh, God, I want to die."

"Sugar—" He moved toward her, his arms outstretched.

She slapped at his hands. "Don't you dare touch me, Flint Durham! I'm furious with you!" So mortified was she to see herself displayed like a *Playboy* bunny that she couldn't even look at the obscenity again.

Suddenly, something struck her as very odd. She forced herself to glance at the nude, then she looked around the room. The oil's color scheme and its heavy frame as well as the placement of the enormous painting gave the impression that it belonged in the room.

Her eyes narrowed.

"Flint, why is that painting in this room and in this house?"

"Babe, I've been meaning to tell you..." he said, taking a step forward.

"Don't call me babe!" She took another step back, caught her foot in the comforter and stumbled. He reached to steady her, but she swatted away his help and hitched up her bulky covering. "And exactly what have you been meaning to tell me?"

"Promise you won't get mad?"

"I promise nothing. But you'd better spit it. Now."

He sucked in a deep breath and slowly blew it out. "This is my room, and this is my house."

Stunned, she stared at him. She didn't think she could get any more angry. She was wrong. He had tricked her. Her Uncle William had tricked her. Everybody in Garner Valley must have been in on the ruse. A blistering heat rose up from her toes.

"You son of a bitch!" Whirling, she stomped from the room, the bulky comforter dragging behind her like a quilted train.

Just as she flung open the door, he grabbed her. "Dammit, Julie, listen to me."

The twins stood right outside the door, wide-eyed and gaping at Julie and Flint.

Julie grabbed the twins and pressed their faces against the puffy fabric. "Don't curse in front of my children, and cover yourself! You're buck naked." Wrestling with her cumbersome sarong, she said, "Don't look, kids," and herded them away.

"Where do you think you're going?" he yelled after her.

"I'm going to pack. And then I'm going to Texas!"

"Julie!" Flint shouted. She ignored him.

"Does this mean that you and Flint aren't going on a honeymoon?" Jason asked.

"It means exactly that."

"Oh, shoot," he groused, "I thought I was finally gonna get a dog."

Julie seethed the entire time it took her to dress and pack her things. She glanced at her watch and saw that the flight she'd booked to Houston would be leaving in three hours, so she hurried to get the children's stuff packed.

In Megan's room, her daughter sat on the side of her bed, her head down, her fingers twisted together. Julie retrieved a suitcase from Megan's closet and opened it on the bed. "Sweetheart, help Mommy get your clothes packed. Empty the drawers while I get Jason started on his things."

She walked through the adjoining bathroom and glanced into Jason's room. He wasn't there. He was probably downstairs. She went back into Megan's room and said, "Where is your brother?"

Megan shrugged her shoulders and looked away.

Julie recognized the gestures. Megan was a terrible fibber. "Megan, I asked you a question. Where is your brother?" she asked sternly.

Megan mumbled something.

"I didn't hear you. Where is Jason?"

"He went to find Old Two Toes."

Julie frowned. "Old Two Toes?"

"Yes. I told him not to go, but he's going to find Old Two Toes and touch his tail and wish we could stay here and wish that you and Flint would go on a honeymoon so he can be our daddy.''

''Jason went up in the mountains alone?''

Megan nodded.

''When?''

''While you were in the shower.''

Julie felt the blood drain from her face. That was almost an hour ago. Jason, her baby who had no sense of direction, was in the mountains alone. She dashed for the stairs, screaming, ''Flint!''

Twelve

Half an hour before, Javier had taken one fork of the trail, and Flint had taken the other. Now Flint was sweating bullets as he rode Gazer up the hills, shouting Jason's name. He cursed himself for ten kinds of fool. First, he'd lied to Julie—or all but lied—when he'd deceived her about the house. When he and William Travis, Julie's uncle and his old fishing buddy and only ally in the Travis family, had cooked up the scheme, it had seemed like a great idea. Of course, William had been half-drunk, and Flint had been madder than a sack full of hornets.

And to cap things off he'd told the twins that dumb story about Old Two Toes. If Jason got hurt, the blame would be laid on Flint's doorstep—and rightly so. Bad things could happen to a kid alone and lost in the mountains or the foothills. There really were a few brown bears around, and if Jason by some chance found one and tried to get close enough to touch its tail— Flint shuddered.

"Jason!" he shouted. "Answer me!"

The only sounds he heard were the sighs of the wind through the trees and the creak of his saddle. If he didn't find the boy in another ten or fifteen minutes, he would signal Julie to call the authorities.

Please, he prayed, *let me find Jason.* If anything happened to that child, he could never live with himself. And any hope of reconciling with Julie would be lost forever.

"Jason!"

What was that? He tensed, straining to listen for the sound.

"Jason!"

There it was again. He nudged Gazer upward, calling.

"Here," came the small voice.

Flint nudged Gazer again in the direction of the voice. As he rounded a bend, there sat Jason atop a rock outcropping.

When he recognized Flint, Jason stood and grinned broadly. "I'm sure glad to see you. Very, very glad."

"Are you okay?"

Jason nodded. "I didn't skin my knee or nothing. I just got lost." He sighed. "I looked and looked for Old Two Toes, but I couldn't find him. Then I couldn't 'member which way to go. Mom said if I got lost, for heaven's sake sit down in one place till somebody finds me. And that's what I did." He lifted his chin smugly, looking extremely proud of himself.

Flint grinned. Something about that kid went straight to his heart and tied it in a thousand knots. "You did the right thing, but your Mom and I were worried about you. You shouldn't ever go off without permission. Let me signal that I've found you, and we'll head back." He took the rifle from its scabbard and fired one shot into the air.

When he replaced the weapon, he scooted back in the saddle, then lifted and plunked Jason in front of him.

"Are you mad at me?" the boy asked, looking up over his shoulder, worry clouding his dark eyes.

Flint smoothed the boy's cowlick, the one that Julie was always trying to control, one very similar to the one that had always plagued him. "No, I'm not mad."

"Good. I don't want you to be mad at me and Megan. We're sorry we waked you up and made Mom yell at you. Is she still mad?"

"I think so. But it's not you that she's angry with, Jason. It's me."

"Did you do something bad?"

Flint sighed. "She thinks so."

"Then you should 'pologize. You should 'pologize and say you're very, very, very sorry and you'll never, never, never do that again, and she'll hug you and say,

'That's all right, pumpkin,' and she won't be mad anymore.''

"I wish it were that simple."

"It is. She's a very nice lady."

"I'll agree with that. Tell me, Jason, why did you go looking for Old Two Toes?"

The child was quiet for a moment, then said, "I wanted to make a wish."

"Bears are very dangerous, you know. If you'd found one, you could have been hurt or killed."

"I know," he said in a tiny voice.

"What did you want so badly, Jason? What were you going to wish for?"

"I was going to wish that you would go on a honeymoon with my mom."

Flint grinned. "So that you could have a German shepherd?"

Jason lay back against Flint's chest. "No, so that you could be our daddy."

Flint tried to speak, but the words couldn't get around the big lump in his throat. After a minute or so, he cleared his throat and said, "Any man would be proud to have you as a son and Megan as a daughter."

Eyes shining, Jason looked up at him and a huge, sunny smile spread over his face. Damned if Flint didn't get another lump in his throat.

As they rode down the trail, Jason touched Flint's hand on the reins. He stroked the little finger and said, "You've got a finger like me. See?"

The boy held up his left hand and, sure enough, the top knuckle of his little finger was permanently bent in exactly the same way as Flint's.

"Mom said I 'herited it from my father. He died in a car wreck when me and Megan was just little babies."

Jason prattled on, but Flint didn't hear a word more. A chill chased down his back, and his breath left him. *Dear, God, was it possible?*

"Tell me, Jason, exactly when is your birthday?" The boy told him. Flint counted back nine months from the day and cursed silently. The twins were conceived long before he left Travis Creek. Even if he allowed for their coming a month early, he came up with the same conclusion.

The twins were his. *He* was Megan and Jason's father.

And Julie hadn't told him.

Anger began to simmer inside him. The closer he got to the house, the more furious he became. Dammit! He had a right to know that he was a father. She was just going to pack her bags and kiss him off for some asinine little fib that didn't amount to a hill of beans, and here she was in a whopper of a lie about his children. *His* children.

He rode Gazer right up to the back patio where Julie, Megan and Alma waited.

"Oh, honey, I've been so worried about you," Julie said. She snatched Jason off the horse, hugged him fiercely and rained kisses over his face.

"Oh, Mom," Jason groused, wrinkling his nose and trying to squirm away from her kisses. "I'm okay."

When she set him down, Flint dismounted and looked at Alma. "Take the children inside for a snack. I need to speak with their mother." Alma, obviously sensing trouble, shooed the children inside.

Flint watched Julie swell up like a toad, then turn and let loose her anger on him. He let her invectives sail right over his head. He was twice as angry as she'd ever been on her best day, but he kept a tight rein on his temper.

"When were you going to tell me?" he asked, his eyes boring into hers.

Her tirade stopped. "Tell you what?"

"That Megan and Jason are mine."

She paled. "What are you talking about?"

"Don't lie to me, Julie. Jason told me when his birthday was. It didn't take a genius to make a simple calculation. I was a fool not to have figured it out before now. I'm their *father*. Dammit, I had a right to know."

Her eyes blazed, and she got in his face. "A right? A *right?* Where were you and your rights when I found out I was pregnant? I'll tell you where!" She poked a finger in his chest. "You were off doing your thing somewhere in California, that's where. But did you tell me where or care what happened to me after you left? Hell, no.

"And where were you when I was in labor for eighteen hours and gave birth to two illegitimate babies alone? Where were you when I walked the floor with two colicky infants, changed endless diapers and sat up nights rocking them when they were sick? Off 'doing your thing,'" she singsonged.

"Flint Durham, don't talk to me about rights! You don't have any rights to my children. You forfeited your rights when you rode off on that damned Harley and left me alone and pregnant!"

"I didn't know you were pregnant."

"Nor did I, Mr. John Anthony Durham. But you know what? I don't think it would have made a damned bit of difference to you. You were hell-bent on following your dream."

Her every word pierced his heart, and he wanted to defend himself, but he clung to his indignation and his pride. "Whatever our past, I am the father of those children," he stormed.

"Only through a biological accident. You have no right to them."

"We'll see about that. I'm not the poor, powerless bastard I used to be. My attorney will be in touch." Before he said something that he would regret, Flint quickly swung into Gazer's saddle and kicked the horse into a gallop toward the hills.

Angry enough to chew light bulbs, Julie strode into the house and headed for the kitchen. Megan and Jason were sitting at the breakfast table with milk and cookies. When Julie yanked a butcher knife from the wooden block on the counter, the twins' eyes widened and they looked at each other.

"What's she gonna do?" Jason asked.

"I don't know," Megan said.

"Surgery," Julie supplied tersely. "Finish your snack and go upstairs and start getting your things together. We're leaving in ten minutes."

She marched to Flint's bedroom and went directly to the painting. Like a thief in the Louvre, she quickly sliced the oil from its frame. She tossed the knife on the bed, rolled up the nude and stuck it under her arm, then snatched up her silk dress and other things and hurried upstairs.

By the time Julie and the twins came downstairs a few minutes later, Javier had returned.

Flint had not.

Which was just fine with her. It seemed that he always rode off at critical times. On a Harley or on a horse, he was gone without a backward glance. And she was left to deal with the fallout.

Well, good riddance.

Javier agreed to drive them to the airport. They could barely make their flight if they hurried. The twins dawdled, whining and giving her a hard time, but she gave them a stern lecture and herded them into the Cherokee as soon as they had said their goodbyes to Alma. Jason insisted on sitting in the front with Javier, so she and Megan sat in the back.

They were the last ones on the flight to Houston. Barely were their seat belts buckled when the plane taxied out to the runway. Jason, who sat next to the window, pressed his face against the glass and watched until the airport was out of sight.

She knew what her son was hoping for, but she didn't want to be cruel and tell him that he couldn't count on seeing Flint again. She planned on dropping out of sight with the kids for a while. Exactly where, she didn't know. Going back to Travis Creek was out. Not only didn't she want to face the town gossips, but she was also angry with her parents and stung by her favorite uncle's betrayal.

The flight had a stop at the Dallas/Fort Worth airport. For a moment she considered getting off and going to her sister Melissa's in Dallas, but Melissa didn't have room for them in her small apartment. Too, she didn't want any of her family to know where she was, not even her sister.

An idea hit her. Sandra Hammond, her roommate from college, lived in Terrell, a small town outside of Dallas. Sandra and her husband, Gil, had bought a huge old home there and had restored it. In her last letter, her friend had sent pictures of the house and the guest cottage and begged her and the twins to come for a visit. Julie had hoped to go before the wedding, but things got hectic and she hadn't made it.

Sandra and Gil had two boys, four and six, and another on the way—which was why they hadn't been able to come to Travis Creek for Julie's nuptials.

Julie searched her purse until she found her address book, then she turned to the *H*'s. Using the phone on the seat back in front of her and a credit card, she soon had Sandra on the phone.

"Julie," her friend squealed. "It's so good to hear from you. Are you already back from your honeymoon?"

"Well, Sandra, a funny thing happened on the way to the altar."

Following Sandra's directions very carefully, Julie managed to find both Terrell and Ashbury Street with only a few minor glitches along the way. She had the twins looking for numbers, Jason on the right and Megan on the left. Although they weren't in kindergarten yet, both children knew the ABCs, could print their names and already knew their numbers up to a hundred. It was of considerable help in circumstances like the present.

"There it is! There it is!" shouted Megan, pointing to the large cream-colored house with an abundance of porches, columns, cornices and dormers.

Julie pulled the rented car into the circular driveway and tooted the horn. The door opened and Sandra, red-haired, seven months' pregnant and her face aglow, hurried out to greet them. The two old friends hugged, and Sandra said hello to the twins, hugging them each in turn.

Matt, the four-year-old, and a long-haired mutt named Fred also bounded out of the house, Matt galloping on an imaginary horse and Fred barking and running in circles around the group.

"Welcome to chaos," Sandra said, laughing. "It gets worse when Skip gets out of school and Gil gets home from work. Pull your car around back to the cottage, and I'll shepherd the kiddos that way. We'll unload your stuff, give the rug rats a plate of cookies on the porch and have a nice long visit. We have a ton of stuff to catch up on—and some of it juicy from the teasers you dropped. God, I'm so glad you're here." Sandra hugged her again.

Julie was glad, too. She felt warm and sheltered and ten pounds lighter just from being around Sandra. She had made the perfect choice in coming here.

Over the next several days, Julie reaffirmed the wisdom of her decision. The cottage was perfect for her and the children, and because it had its own kitchen, she didn't feel as if she were imposing on Sandra and her family. The twins loved having playmates like Skip and Matt and their friends, and their constant activity kept them from dwelling on leaving Garner Valley and Flint.

Julie called Melissa to tell her that she and the kids were okay and asked her sister to pass the word to the family. No, she wouldn't tell Melissa where she was, but she would be checking in every few days if there was an emergency.

Sharing coffee in the morning or tea in the afternoon, Julie gradually confided in Sandra about her problems with Flint. As she suspected, Sandra was totally empathetic and nonjudgmental.

"You should see the look in your eyes when you talk about Flint," Sandra said. "I think you're still in love with him."

Julie sighed. "I don't think ... I know. I guess I've always been in love with him even though I wouldn't admit it. But some things just aren't meant to be. I have too much bitterness inside, and he's angry that he's been deprived of his children. If only we'd had a little more time together before he found out about the twins, maybe we could have worked things out."

"Couldn't you still try?"

"Not with the threat of his taking the children hanging over my head. I couldn't risk it." Julie felt tears sting her eyes and tried to blink them away. They spilled over despite her best efforts. "Oh, darn," she said, grabbing a tissue. "I hate crying, and I seem to be doing it all the time."

Sandra hugged her and rubbed her back. "I'm so sorry, sweetie. Sometimes love can be a real bitch."

Julie laughed, blew her nose and took a last sip of her cooling coffee.

Flint took another swig of Jack Daniel's and stared at the bare spot where the painting of Julie had been. He'd never been much of a drinker because of his father's alcoholism, but Flint had gone through a lot of Jack Daniel's in the past three weeks.

Drinking didn't help much, but neither did anything else. He'd split three cords of wood for the fireplace. Every day he swam laps in the pool until he was exhausted, then rode Gazer until they were both blowing hard. He'd bought a new Harley, thinking to take to the mountain roads and outrun the devil on his tail, but when he looked at the damned thing, he remembered the mess he'd made of Julie's life by riding off on a Harley, then riding back in and screwing up her wedding.

It was damned hard to fill up the days. The nights were hell. So he drank. To forget. To dull the pain. To self-destruct.

Kyle Rutledge walked in, leaned against the dresser and thumbed back the white cowboy hat he always wore. "What are you doing in here?"

"Wallowing in my misery."

"You look like dog puke."

Flint toasted him with the whisky bottle. "I feel like dog puke." He took another swig. "Join me for a drink? I think there's an extra bottle on the chest."

"I'll pass. But I wouldn't mind a home-cooked meal. Alma made a pot roast and it's on the table."

"She call you?"

"Alma's worried that you haven't been eating properly." Kyle nodded to the half-empty bottle. "And that stuff is going to kill you. Come on, let's go sop up some of that alcohol with mashed potatoes."

"I'll pass." Flint turned up the bottle again.

"Dammit, man, why don't you call her? Tell her what a jerk you are and throw yourself on her mercy."

"I have called. I've called her snooty parents. I've called her uncle. I've called her sister. I've called her preacher. Nobody knows where she is. Or if they do, they're not telling. Hell, I've even hired a private detective. It's as if Julie and the kids have dropped off the face of the earth.''

''She's in hiding. You shouldn't have threatened to take her kids.''

''I know that. Hell, I didn't even mean it at the time. I was just mad and shot my mouth off. Really, I was more mad at myself than at her.'' The bottle dropped to the floor, and the bourbon glugged onto the carpet. With his elbows propped on his knees, he held his head in his hands. ''Julie is the only thing I've ever cared about in this sorry life of mine, and I've screwed up big-time. Hell, six years ago, I ran off and left her pregnant. And Travis Creek isn't Hollywood. Unwed mothers might as well be branded. No wonder she hated me. And I tricked her into coming here. I'm a sorry—''

''Son of a bitch,'' Kyle finished for him. ''I agree. Now what are you going to do about it?''

''There's nothing I can do.''

''Bull. There's always something you can do. You're just too drunk to think.'' Kyle dragged Flint to his feet. ''Come on. Let's get some coffee and food in you.''

The minute Flint stood, his stomach rolled, and he felt green all over. ''I—I'd better stop by the bathroom. I think I'm going to be sick.''

Thirteen

"Julie, what's wrong?" Sandra asked, sounding alarmed as she rushed in the bathroom.

"Ohh. I've never been so sick in my life."

"How long has this been going on?"

"For two or three days. Ohh, I'm dying. I must be. Ohh, God."

"Hush, Julie, your carrying on is frightening the twins. You're not dying. I suspect what's ailing you will become apparent fairly soon."

"You can't mean—"

Sandra nodded. "I suspect Flint is the reason you're tossing your cookies."

"Oh, dear Lord, no. It can't be. I'll die. I'll just die."

"*Che sarà, sarà*, sweetie. Come on. You need to eat a few crackers and lie down for a moment."

The twins stood outside the bathroom door, looking extremely disturbed. "What's wrong with Mommy?" Megan asked Sandra as she helped Julie.

"Just an upset tummy. Why don't you two go in the yard and play on the swings until your mom is feeling better."

Jason and Megan sat on the swings but they weren't swinging. "Jason, I'm scared. Mommy is sick, very, very sick."

"Dying," he added, "and throwing up awful."

"And she cries all the time when she thinks we're not around."

"She misses Flint."

"I do, too."

"Me, too."

"If Flint was here, he'd know how to make Mommy well."

"Maybe we should call him."

"And just how you gonna do that, Jason? We don't got his telephone number."

He shot her a smug grin. "I do."

"Where?" she asked, not believing her brother for one second.

"In my backpack. In my room. Come on. I'll show you."

They ran back to the cottage and opened the door very quietly and tiptoed to Jason's room. Jason got down on his knees and dragged his backpack from under the bed. He unzipped one of the pockets and pulled out something.

"That's a cell'ar phone, Jason! Where did you get that?"

"Shh. I got it out of the glove compartment of the Jeep. When we was going to the airport."

"Mmm-mmm, Jason. That's stealing. Pure-dee stealing."

"Shh. No it's not. It's borr'ing. And I'm glad I borr'ed it. When me and you and Mom got lost, and we had a 'mergency and had to call Flint and Dr. Kyle to come get us in the helicopter, how did we call Flint?"

Megan's eyes widened and a grin spread over her face. "On the cell'ar phone."

"Yep. On this cell'ar phone. And I 'member how she done it."

"How she *did* it."

"Yep. She punched this button, and then this button, and then Flint said hello."

"I know how to do it," Megan said. "It's just like the one Mommy has at home. On hers when you punch this button, it rings at home and Rosie answers, and if you punch this button, it rings Uncle William, and if you punch this button—"

Jason yanked the phone away from his sister. "I don't care about that stuff. This one rings Flint. I'm gonna call him." He punched the buttons, put the phone to his ear and waited. And waited. "Nothin' happens."

Megan listened. "I think we gotta hook it up to the car first." She held up the wire dangling from the phone.

They sneaked outside and very quietly opened the door of the car they got from the airport. Once inside, Jason pulled out the cigarette lighter and plugged in the phone.

"Look!" Megan cried when the phone lit up.

Jason pushed the two buttons and waited for a long time. "It's ringing!" When someone answered he said, "Alma, is that you? This is Jason. Is Flint there? Yes, I'll wait." He covered the phone and said to Megan, "She got all 'cited and said to wait. I'm waitin'."

"Jason! This is Flint. Son, where are you?"

"We're at the little house behind Aunt Sandra's big house. Only she's not really our aunt. She's Mom's very good friend. Her and Uncle Gil. Only he's not our uncle. Me and Megan was callin' because Mom's sick. Real sick. She's very, very sick. Dying, I think. And she cries a lot and her face gets spotted. Megan is scared, and we want you to come. I miss you somethin' awful."

"Tell him I miss him too," Megan whispered.

"Megan said she misses you, too. I took the cell'ar phone out of the Jeep, and that's how I'm callin' you. Are you mad I took it?"

"No, Jason. I'm glad you took it."

"When can you come? Mom is real sick. She's dying for sure."

"I'll be there as soon as I can, but you have to tell me where to come. What town are you in?"

"What town are we in, Megan?"

"Terrell, Texas."

"Flint, we're—"

"I heard. What street?"

"What street?"

Megan shrugged her shoulders. "I don't remember, but the number on the house is 618."

They couldn't supply Sandra and Gil's last name, nor their phone number, but they described the house and the neighborhood, including the ugly house across the street that Aunt Sandra said was the color of baby poop.

"Kids, I'll be there tomorrow. And I'll find you if I have to drive up and down every street in town."

"Bye, Flint." Jason looked at his sister, grinned and stuck out his hand for a high-five.

"I think we'd better keep this secret," Megan said.

Jason nodded and pulled the plug from the lighter.

Fourteen

Julie had just put two fish sticks on Jason's plate when someone banged on the front door. She quickly spooned on green beans, as well, and served the twins' lunch before she went to see who the caller was.

The banging persisted, louder. "Just a minute," she shouted, licking stickiness from the sweet potato off her thumb as she hurried to the front of the house.

When she opened the door and saw Flint there, she was stunned. He looked very grim. Her heart stumbled, then began beating furiously. "What—"

"Oh, babe, I got here as fast as I could." He rushed in the door and gathered her into his arms. "Have you seen a doctor? What does he say? Whatever it is, we'll get the finest specialists. We'll take you to the Mayo

Clinic.'' He cupped her face in his big hands and kissed her gently. ''Now that I'm here you don't have to worry about a thing. I'll take care of the kids, and you can concentrate on getting well.'' He kissed her forehead. ''I'd die myself if anything happened to you. What are you doing up? Shouldn't you be in bed?''

Julie struggled from his arms. ''What are you talking about? Are you drunk or crazy? How did you find me, and what are you doing here? If you think you're going to take the twins away from me, you've got another think coming, buster! I'll fight you tooth and toenail.''

''Julie, shh, honey, don't get upset. I'm not going to take the twins away from you. I want all of you, a package-deal family.'' He lifted her into his arms, carried her to the couch and sat down with her. His dark eyes scanning her features over and over, he stroked her face as if it were fine porcelain. ''I'm sorry that I was such a dumb jerk. God, I've been going crazy without you. I love you so much that I can't even begin to tell you how miserable I've been. I've phoned everybody I could think of—I even called your parents—trying to find you.''

Amused at the notion of Flint talking with her parents, she said, ''That must have been an interesting conversation.''

''I'm pretty sure that I'm still not on their A-list. But that's not important. I don't give a damn if your parents like me or not. The important thing is how you feel.'' He laid his fingers across her forehead. ''Do you have fever?''

''No, I don't have fever! Are you sure you're not drunk?''

''I've been sober as a judge since Jason called. Babe, I would have been here sooner—I swear I would have—but it took me a while to find a house the color of baby poop. One of the city cops finally—''

''Whoa! *Jason* called you? When?''

''Uh-oh,'' a small voice said from behind the doorway. ''We're in for it now.''

After the twins were asleep, Julie and Flint sat on the wooden swing and moved slowly back and forth. Only a distant street lamp and the soft glow of a gaslight behind the Hammonds' house provided illumination, and the end of the porch where they sat was blanketed by subtle shadows.

The sweetness of Sandra's roses mixed with the scents from her herb garden and wafted through the tranquil night. Julie was cuddled in Flint's arms, feeling for the first time in a long, long time that all was right with the world. Sandra, sharp lady that she was, had insisted that the twins join her boys for a long outing that afternoon. Julie and Flint had spent most of that time talking, really talking.

Communicating.

Julie had been able to, at last, lay her bitterness aside and understand that Flint would never have left her if he had known that she was pregnant. It was her

mother's misguided interference that had done the
most damage. And she tried to understand that Flint's
needs and his perceptions were different from hers
because of his background. Because she'd never been
poor or abused, she couldn't fully appreciate the mo-
tivation that drove him to succeed.

He had laid his soul bare to her, and she had done
the same, sharing with him her innermost feelings.
She'd told him everything.

Well, almost everything.

Julie's forehead rested on Flint's cheek, and he
rubbed her arm slowly, setting off lovely little sensa-
tions over her skin. "Flint, what are you thinking?"

"I'm thinking that I'm glad you only had an upset
stomach and weren't dying. But I'm also glad that
Megan and Jason got scared enough to call me. We
came awfully close to losing something wonderful."

"Do you still want to marry me?"

He kissed a spot over her eyebrow. "You betcha.
The sooner, the better."

"Flint?"

"Hmm?"

"How do you feel about being a father?"

"Great. Just great. Megan and Jason are fantastic
kids. You've done a fine job with them."

"No, I meant how to you feel about us having other
children?"

He hesitated. "How do you feel about it?"

"I asked you first."

"Well, honestly, I think I'd like it. I missed some special times when Megan and Jason were babies. It would be sort of neat to be around when your kid is born and takes his first steps, that kind of thing."

"I'm glad you feel that way, because I'm pretty sure you're going to have a chance to do those things."

Flint stiffened. "What do you mean?"

"I think my upset tummy was morning sickness. And unless the home pregnancy test I took this morning is wrong, it looks like you're going to be a father about next Valentine's Day."

"You're kidding?"

She chuckled. "Nope. You are one virile son of a gun."

Flint shot out of the swing, thrust his arms in the air, threw back his head and yelled, "Waaaaaa-hooooo!"

"Flint!" Julie admonished, laughing and trying to cover his mouth. "Hush. You'll rouse the neighborhood."

"Good." He grabbed her and spun her around. "Then I can announce to the whole bunch of them that—" he cupped his hands around his mouth and shouted "—we're going to have a baby!" He kissed her and spun her around some more. Then he stopped. "Is it just one, or are we going to have twins again?"

"It's too soon to tell."

"Maybe it'll be triplets. Wouldn't that be something? Come on. Let's go to bed and celebrate. Do you know what I want to do to you?" He slowly circled the shell of her ear with his tongue, then whispered some extremely erotic suggestions.

Julie laughed. "Flint Durham, that's indecent."

"Wanna do it, anyway?"

"I'm game."

They locked the door to Julie's bedroom and had a very adventurous night.

The wedding was planned for three days later in Sandra's rose garden. Two high school boys spent most of Saturday morning sprucing up the yard, and Gil borrowed folding chairs from the local funeral parlor. The assistant pastor of the Hammonds' church, who happened to be a lovely woman and a grandmother of six, would perform the ceremony. Afterward, the wedding party would have cake—provided by the local Brookshire Brothers bakery department—and champagne—courtesy of William Travis—on the Hammonds' veranda. The members of Sandra's bridge club had gathered enough champagne glasses and plates to serve everyone.

Julie's wedding dress was blue—because Flint liked her in blue—and it was outrageously expensive—because Flint said he could damn well afford for his bride to have the prettiest dress to be found in Neiman Marcus. And anyway, he owed her for tearing up her last one.

In the cottage Julie held out her dress and twirled around. "How do I look?" she asked Melissa.

"Fantastic. Like Cinderella at the ball. Like the happiest bride I've ever seen."

"That's because I *am* the happiest bride. Oh, Melissa, I love him so. I just wish Mother and Daddy would accept that."

"They're here, aren't they? That's a step in the right direction. And really, they both want you to be happy. Marrying Rob would have been a big mistake, wouldn't it?"

"Yes, a very big one. I feel awful about him. He's such a nice man, but he just wasn't for me."

Melissa casually wound a lock of hair around her finger and glanced away. "How do you think he would be for me?"

Julie frowned. "What do you mean?"

"Would you be upset if I dated Rob?"

"Why, no. Of course not."

Melissa grinned. "Good, because I'm crazy about him, and we've been going out a lot."

The sisters hugged. "I'm delighted. I think you're perfect for each other," Julie told her.

"Is my tie straight?" Flint asked Kyle.

They had dressed in one of the guest rooms at the big house and were waiting to go downstairs and take their places by the garden bench.

"Just as straight as it was when you asked me the same thing two minutes ago. Are you nervous, pal?"

"Can you tell?"

Kyle laughed. "Do ducks fly? Why in the world are you nervous? You're getting everything you wanted. A beautiful woman that you love and two great kids."

"I'm afraid some damned fool is going to roar in and screw up the wedding. God is good about getting his licks in."

"I think God is tickled to death that the two of you are finally getting together."

Flint looked in the mirror to check on his tie again. Damned thing looked crooked to him. "Kyle, I sure do appreciate your coming to be my best man. I know it must have played hell with your schedule."

"Naw," Kyle said. "I wouldn't have missed this occasion for the world. Anyway, I never pass up an excuse to visit Texas. I miss it, you know."

"Texas?"

Kyle nodded. "I've never quite adjusted to California." He glanced at his watch. "It's time."

"Is my tie straight?"

The Hammonds' next-door neighbor's daughter-in-law had volunteered to play the harp. When the first dulcet tones floated from the strings and reverberated beneath the umbrella of ancient oak and pecan trees, the entire garden was transformed into an enchanted place. The rippling notes fluttered like fairies scattering gold dust across the lawn.

Flint and Kyle stood by the stone bench with the pastor. Julie, holding a bouquet of white roses and orchids, stood beside her father on the cottage porch.

George Travis smiled. "Nervous?"

"Not at all. This time I'm marrying the right man."

He patted her hand. "I hope so, sweetheart. Your mother and I only want the best for you."

"I have the best, Daddy. Believe me."

"Say, I understand that Flint knows my favorite film star."

When her father named the leading man of Flint's movies, Julie chuckled. "Yes, he knows him very well. Have you seen *Bad Blues Heat* and *Bad Blues Heat II?*"

"Certainly. I have all his movies on video tape."

"Next time you watch them, check out the credits for who wrote the screenplay. Oops, we're about to begin."

Megan and Jason led the procession. Jason carried a pillow with gold rings tied securely atop it and walked very carefully down the path to the bench. As he neared, he grinned at his father, and Flint winked.

Megan came next, her new dress the same shade of blue as her mother's. She scattered rose petals from an Easter basket Sandra had retrieved from the attic and decorated with a satin bow. Megan didn't have to worry about running out of petals. The day before, Flint had bought all the roses that two florists and a road-side vendor had so that Megan could pluck them and put them into the refrigerator. She scattered petals munificently and was in absolute heaven.

Watching her children, Julie's heart swelled with joy and pride. How she loved them! And how she loved their father.

As soon as Melissa took her place, the melody of the harp changed. Julie's father kissed her cheek, and they started walking slowly toward the stone bench where Flint and the others waited.

Uncle William sat on the second row, grinning broadly. Julie gave him a subtle thumbs-up as she passed.

When she and her father reached their destination, they stopped and the pastor began. "Who gives this woman..."

After her father had said the proper words and stepped away, she and Flint joined hands. She looked up to see his dark eyes shining with all the love that she'd ever hoped to find. And his smile was for her alone.

Suddenly, they heard the loud roar of an engine. It split the quiet like a buzz saw and shattered the enchantment of the ceremony.

Julie gasped.

Flint groaned softly and almost squeezed her fingers off.

Slowly they turned and glanced over their shoulders.

The man who lived in the mustard-colored house wielded a gasoline lawn edger along the front curb that belched smoke and spewed a raucous drone that could be heard for two blocks.

Nervous titters rippled through the gathering. Gil took off across the street at a fast trot. In a few moments, quiet reigned again and the ceremony continued without a hitch.

Julie and Flint pledged their vows in strong, clear voices. At last the pastor said, "You may kiss the bride."

Flint gently encircled her in his arms and kissed her sweetly. The guests applauded, and everyone laughed. The informal ceremony was done.

"On the *mouth*," Jason whispered to his sister. "Yuck."

"I think it's wonderful," Megan said. "They do all that kissin' and go on a honeymoon. You know what that means."

A slow smile spread over Jason's face. "Yeah. I'm gonna get a dog."

"And I'm going to get a kitty. A white one. I'm going to name her Snowflake."

"Mine is gonna be a German shepherd named Rex."

While Jason and Megan ate wedding cake and played chase with Matt and Skip, a white Persian kitten and a German shepherd puppy were already waiting in Garner Valley for their master and mistress to come home.

* * * * *

The collection of the year!
NEW YORK TIMES BESTSELLING AUTHORS

Linda Lael Miller
Wild About Harry

Janet Dailey
Sweet Promise

Elizabeth Lowell
Reckless Love

Penny Jordan
Love's Choices

and featuring
Nora Roberts
The Calhoun Women

This special trade-size edition features four of the wildly popular titles in the Calhoun miniseries together in one volume—a true collector's item!

Pick up these great authors and a chance to win a weekend for two in New York City at the Marriott Marquis Hotel on Broadway! We'll pay for your flight, your hotel—even a Broadway show!

Available in December at your favorite retail outlet.

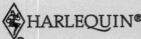 

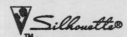

*'Tis the season for
holiday weddings!*

This December, celebrate the holidays
with two sparkling new love stories—
only from

A Nice Girl Like You
by Alexandra Sellers

Sara Diamond may be a nice girl, but that doesn't mean
she wants to be Ben Harris's ideal bride. But she might
just be able to play Ms. Wrong long enough to help this
confirmed bachelor find his true wife! That is, if she
doesn't fall in love first....

A Marry-Me Christmas
by Jo Ann Algermissen

All Catherine Jordan wanted for Christmas was some
time away from the hustle and bustle. Now she was
sharing a wilderness cabin with her infuriating opposite,
Stone Scofield! But once she stood under the mistletoe
with Stone, she was hoping for a whole lot more
this holiday....

Don't miss these exciting new books,
our gift to you this holiday season!

Look us up on-line at: http://www.romance.net

XMASYT

Concluding in November from Silhouette books...

This exciting new cross-line continuity series unites five
of your favorite authors as they weave five connected
novels about love, marriage—and Daddy's unexpected
need for a baby carriage!

You fell in love with the wonderful characters in:

THE BABY NOTION by Dixie Browning (Desire 7/96)

BABY IN A BASKET by Helen R. Myers
(Romance 8/96)

MARRIED...WITH TWINS! by Jennifer Mikels
(Special Edition 9/96)

HOW TO HOOK A HUSBAND (AND A BABY)
by Carolyn Zane (Yours Truly 10/96)

And now all of your questions will finally be answered in

DISCOVERED: DADDY
by Marilyn Pappano (Intimate Moments 11/96)

Everybody is still wondering...who's the father of prim and
proper Faith Harper's baby? But Faith isn't letting anyone
in on her secret—not until she informs the daddy-to-be.
Trouble is, *he* doesn't seem to remember her....

Don't miss the exciting conclusion of
DADDY KNOWS LAST...only in Silhouette books!

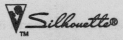